Sugar Princess

NICOLINA MARTIN

Edited by Nerine Dorman

Cover by Dani René

Chapter One

Tommaso

The store is no more than a hole in the wall, and the whole front is floor-to-ceiling windows that don't cover much of what goes on inside. I shake my head. Those windows could easily shatter if I wanted to, say, get the owner's attention.

Inside the store, a young woman moves between mismatched armchairs of various sizes and little round tables crowded too close together. Behind the chairs and tables are shelves filled to the brim with books of all sizes. Hardcovers, paperbacks, and coffee table books, passionately squeezed in to fit as many as possible in a seemingly unsystematic manner. There's love behind the arrangement. That pleases me. I appreciate reading. It's weightlifting for my mind, and I like staying in shape. The messy display offends my sense of order, though. I would have organized it differently.

Rounded, pink neon letters along the façade spell out 'Sugar Princess'. An arc is painted on the window in several shades of pastel: 'Sweet Heroes and Spicy Heroines. We have a flavor for everyone.'

I don't understand the shop's concept. Is it a bookstore or a café? Well, it's not my business. I'm here to collect. I kick down the support and jerk up my motorcycle so that it locks in place, then I pocket the key and march up to the door. Collecting protection money was something I did when I was twelve. At thirty-nine, I thought those days were past, but thanks to my *idiota* drunk of a brother, here I am again, stuck in the US of A for a few months, paying off his debt.

Back then, I would go in with a bat, smash up some shelves and break a few things. It usually did the trick. Today, I hope to settle this with a few well-considered words. I pull open the door, step inside, and take a deep breath. To my surprise, I'm met by the sweet smell of vanilla, like from panna cotta, my favorite dessert, and not musty books, as expected.

The girl by the tables freezes with her back to me. I raise an eyebrow, appreciating her outfit. A wide, brown leather belt nips in her small waist, creating an alluring hour-glass shape. Below the belt, a wide, deep red skirt falls to her knees. Above the belt, a red-and-white polka dot blouse stretches across her ample chest. As she turns to me, I must drag my gaze away from the creamy skin of her breasts revealed by the blouse's plunging neckline. Her honey-blond hair is tied into two braids that rest, one in front, and the other behind her shoulders. On top of her head sits a glittering tiara, worthy of a princess. She widens her round blue eyes as she lets them travel my body, and her intense scrutiny is an almost physical sensation. She looks as taken aback as I feel myself.

Her heart-shaped face opens into a smile that reveals deep dimples. What do they say, the Americans? Cute as pie. To my Italian soul she is cute as the sweet pudding this whole bookstore smells of.

"How do you do, sir?" she asks, pulling me out of the near trance.

Sir.

I like how polite she is. I hope she's as pliable as she is polite and will fold like a cheap lawn chair when I put pressure on her. It would be a shame to have to wreck this little shop.

"Is that coffee I smell?" I remove my sunglasses and move a step closer. She backs up. Her instincts tell her something is wrong, but the polite veneer doesn't wear off just because everything inside her screams at her to be careful. She works in retail, and I am a customer.

"Y-yeah," she stutters as a blush creeps up the sides of her cheeks. "I just put it on. It will be a few minutes. Did… did you come here looking for something special?"

I sure did, and she's not going to like it one bit.

Carrie

"What is your name?" His deep baritone combined with a thick accent I can't pinpoint, maybe southern European, possibly Italian, causes a shiver to run through me. He is made up of squares, I decide: a squared jaw, squared shoulders, a squared forehead. His thick dark hair lies neatly combed back, tamed with hair gel, light green penetrating eyes that flash as they look me over, and a massive black beard. He looks like someone glued a suit onto a caveman. Primitive. Capable. Sexy as all hell.

I haven't been with a man for two years. Not since my father passed, and I kicked Ethan out.

Ethan is the most self-centered person I have ever known, and he somehow managed to make my grief all about himself. Having given him eight years already, that was the last straw.

I haven't looked at a man since. I've kept my head down and worked.

But today I not only look, I gawk.

Something about this rough stranger with his expensive-looking suit, and his intense gaze, has me spellbound. The silence is deafening. I realize I'm staring, and that he asked me a question.

"Ehm... Carrie. Carrie Ellerbrock."

"And are you from California, Carrie Ellerbrock?" It sounds as if his tongue is making love with my name, and I choke down the moan that wants to climb up my throat. Italian, I decide. That raw, sexy accent is definitely Italian.

I can't tear my gaze off his hands as he slowly pulls off his black leather gloves, meticulously, finger by finger. His hands are callused, huge, deliciously veiny squares, too. Jesus Christ. My girl parts clench from the vision before me, and my mind plunges into the gutter with a dizzying speed as I imagine what those rough palms could do to my bottom.

"Mm-hmm."

His gloves held in one hand, he pulls off his coat, hangs it over one arm and then moves, seemingly regarding the bookshelves. This gives me a perfect opportunity to study his broad back.

"And is this your business, Miss Ellerbrock?"

The silence mounts between us. I'm supposed to answer? This is ridiculous. How can anyone be expected to function when sex on legs walks into their little bookstore? The coffee brewer gurgles, signaling that the last few drops are hitting the pot, pulling me out of my weird hypnotized state.

I clear my throat, square my shoulders, and involuntarily jut out my substantial bust, but lose the ability to speak when his gaze lands on my breasts.

"Mmph," I say then flee to the safety behind the

counter, aiming for the coffee pot and the rack with cups. His presence burns holes in my back as I pour a cup of coffee, shaking slightly. I ground myself in the familiarity of the action, and as I turn back to him, my hands are steady again.

"Cream or sugar?"

"Black."

Chapter Two

Carrie

He has somehow soundlessly crossed the distance from where he stood in a matter of seconds. I swallow the gasp that wants to escape me, look over his shoulder, at the abandoned street, and then back up at the man, realizing two things: I'm alone with a stranger whom I somehow doubt is here for the classics, and he smells really good.

"Black coffee it is. Do you want anything to go with it?" I scan the assortment of cookies I have yet to unwrap and then I work on routine, unveiling the trays in the cooler counter.

He takes the cup and puts it to his lips, sips, then seems to fight off a shudder as he sets the cup back down on the plate. He glances around, then his eyes land on me again. "You are a little young to be running a business all by yourself, Miss Ellerbrock."

"I'm not that young," I snap back with a laugh. I only look it because I'm cuddly and have these rosy round cheeks I hate. "Did you want something with your coffee?"

"No, thank you, miss. Though the smell is delicious, I admit."

"Can I help you with something? Did you come here looking for a book?"

Do huge, hot, quite scary-looking Italians read romance?

"No." He takes another sip. "I did not come here for the books, but yes, Miss Ellerbrock, you can help me with something."

The way he keeps saying my name makes me swoon, but a dark hunger burns in his eyes that makes me increasingly jittery. He's watching me like a predator ready to pounce his prey.

"Am I making you nervous, little one?"

Aaaand he's seeing right through me.

Yikes.

The way he says 'little one' makes me want to cuddle up and purr despite my inner turmoil. I swallow back the emotion that suddenly threatens to overwhelm me. I was forced to grow up way too early when Mom died, and I became the woman of the house. I took care of my father more than he took care of me, and we were both left with holes in our hearts that we never talked about.

This massive caveman, with his heated gaze, calling me 'little one', makes me want to curl up in his lap, makes me want to be taken care of, for once. How does he do that with a mere few words?

Yes, he's making me nervous. He's rocking my whole freaking existence, pulling up things I'd rather stay buried.

And it's only ten in the morning on a Tuesday.

"Of course not," I say lightly, faking it hard, while my cheeks grow hotter by the second.

"Are you here all alone? Are you not worried something would happen to you? A cute little store like this? It looks like you have put a lot of hard work into it. A lonely girl like yourself. What if a big, bad wolf comes and huffs and puffs your house down?"

I interlace my fingers and lean on my forearm on the counter, toward him. "I know how to defend myself."

"Do you now? And how would you do that? If someone were to take something of value to you, how would you defend that?" He reaches for me and pulls the tiara out of my hair.

It's such a sudden movement, I'm totally unprepared for it. I grasp for my tiara, my heart shooting to my throat. "Hey! Give it back!"

He holds it up, out of reach, and turns it in his hands, looking it over. "Art deco. The roaring twenties. Pretty piece for a pretty *principessa*. Where did you get it?"

I try to reach for his arm, unease crawling in my chest. "Give it back, please!"

"This is of value to you?"

"Yes!" My eyes burn hot with tears I fight to hold back. "Come on. This isn't cool."

The tiara has been in my family for generations. My great grandmother wore it when she got married to a prince, somewhere in Europe, and became a bona fide princess. I grew up with the stories, and the shop's name is inspired by her life. When my father died, he passed it on to me. It pains me that I probably won't have anyone to give it to when I die.

I'm too awkward. I have no hope of ever finding a man that would want to settle with *me*.

And now, this infuriating brute has it.

Standing, he takes a few steps back, holding out the arm with the tiara, making a sweeping gesture around the venue. "Much like your pretty little shop, then, Carrie Ellerbrock. It would be a shame if something happened to it."

"What are you talking about?" I inch toward the phone beneath the counter, hoping he won't notice.

"There are people who can protect you, Carrie, but at a cost."

I move my arm, slowly, so as to avoid raising his suspicions, my heart thundering. "What people?

What cost? The only one who's threatening me right now is you. Please give me back my tiara, sir."

"Everything has a cost, little one. There is a cost of two hundred American dollars to keep you and your precious little shop safe. I'm sure you understand."

"Two hundred— Two hundred... what? What is this? Protection money? This is bullshit!"

"A week," he says.

I've had it. My body sizzles with worried energy, my mind tilts, and my knees feel like jelly when I reach for the phone and tap nine and one holding my finger ready to press the last digit. "I would like for you to give me back my tiara and leave my property. Now. Or I'm calling the cops."

He moves like a big cat, wild and lethal. One moment he's standing a few feet away, with a counter between us, the next he has bridged the gap, jumped the counter, and has me pressed up against the wall. I choke out a surprised gasp, the shock of him slamming into me makes me lose my breath. One hand is wrapped around my chin, but his hand is so large it covers half my face. His other hand crushes my hand with the phone, squeezing my fingers so tightly that tears spring up in my eyes. He slams my arm against the wall. Once. Twice, then he rips the phone out of my hand and spins me around, pressing me cheek first against the ungiving surface of my office door.

"Do. Not. Ever. Threaten me, little *principessa*. Do you know who I am?"

I try to shake my head. Tears stream down my cheeks, and my brain feels like it's been doused with gasoline and set on fire. All I know for sure is that I'll die. I have a massive wall of muscles squeezing me flat against the door. An Italian-accented, deliciously scented wall of muscles.

"Please don't hurt me," I whimper.

"You've been a bad girl," he whispers, his lips brushing my ear when he speaks. A flash of heat rushes down the side of my neck from where he touched.

And it's not the only place that heats up. He's saying it just right, just the way I've always needed to hear it.

"No."

"Oh, yes. Do you know what I do to bad little girls?"

That heat, that molten lava that has centered in my chest, floods between my legs. Oh no, no. This is not turning me on. There are so many wrongs in this scenario, I can't even begin to count them. I fight it, but my heartbeat betrays me, my gasping breaths.

He fiddles with something next to us, and the next moment the door falls open, and we stumble into my office. The door kicked shut behind us, he herds me step by step up against the massive mahogany desk, my father's old desk. I back up, he follows, I back up again, he follows.

"No, please." I shake my head. "Please leave. I'll pay the money!" My voice breaks pathetically.

I'm suddenly overwhelmingly aware of the danger I'm in. I'm alone with a man who clearly doesn't have good intentions, who has threatened me, who looks like he can snap me in two with a flick of his fingers. I glance over at the far corner, at the stairs that lead down to the kitchen and to where Cookie, my neighbor's huge Rottweiler, rests. Tied up, sadly. I should have brought her up to the store with me, except she goes after the sweets and gets underfoot. And she's so good-natured, she'd probably be licking the scary, delicious-smelling man even while he's threatening me. But I'd do anything for the illusion of her protection right now.

He glances to where I'm looking, then scoffs. "I don't care about the money. I care about you calling the cops on me. That"—he spins me around so that I'm facing the desk—"can not"—smack, I'm pushed face first, flush against the chilly wooden surface—"go unpunished." He pulls up my skirt to my waist in one quick move and slaps his huge palm against my ass.

The shock of the impact makes me lose my breath. I gasp for air then cry out as the pain hits me like a freight train. "Ow!"

His hand descends again, smacks against my panty-clad bottom. I scream and squirm.

"Get off me! Ow!"

Smack.

"Let me go!"

Smack.

"Oowww!"

Smack.

"Little girls"—*smack*—"with tiaras"—*smack*—"and pretty little skirts"—*smack*—"do best to do as they're told."

My ass is on fire, set ablaze by his relentless hand. Tears and snot dribble from my face, and I'm waiting for the moment when he pulls down my panties and rapes me. I'm so numb from pain I don't feel that he's stopped.

Once he's pulled down my skirt from where it's been bunched up around my waist, he then helps me stand with a hand supporting my elbow. He's too close, and I don't dare to look up at him. Gently, he cups my cheeks, rubs his thumbs under my eyes, collecting my tears. He rests a finger under my chin, as if wanting to raise my head, but leaving me with the choice.

But I can't.

My mind is a jumbled mess, and I can't look him in those beautiful green eyes and risk that he sees my shame.

He spanked me.

Hard.

I can't believe he did that. My hottest, most forbidden fantasies, all presented to me by a monster in a suit who suddenly invaded my whole existence. It's all so wrong.

He moves, puts something on my head, strokes my hair and then wraps a loose strand around his finger, tugging slightly.

"I don't like to see tears on your face, *bella*. You should never have a reason to cry again." Then he turns and leaves.

The door falls closed. From below comes nonstop barking from poor Cookie, going crazy after hearing me wailing. I put a hand on my head and touch my tiara that he replaced, then I fall to my knees and wail.

"*Ow*! Owowowowowow!"

Chapter Three

Tommaso

I try to tell myself it is nothing but a twist of fate that we met, and a temporary lack of judgment, that made me punish little Miss Ellerbrock in such a manner, but I know it's more. My palm burns from the memory of her soft skin, and I'm finding it increasingly difficult to care about the politics of the local gangsters when all I want is to return to the vanilla-scented girl with the innocent eyes.

"Got the cash from the run?"

I pull myself out of my fantasies and look down at the leader. These are new players on the field. They're young, and they're angry, not to be toyed with. I know this, and yet I can't seem to take them seriously. After digging out my wallet from my pocket, I count the cash while something inside me dies from embarrassment, then I slap a wad of bills into the leader's palm, waiting in silence while he counts.

"You're missing one. Did ya run into trouble?"

I don't know why I do it. I remove my personal wallet, pull out two one-hundred-dollar bills, and add them to the pile. "No problem."

He narrows his eyes and tightens his lips. He looks every inch the psychopath he's rumored to be. "Better be no trouble you ain't tellin' me."

"Not an issue," I say lightly. "You point me where to go, and I'll collect."

He holds my gaze a little while longer then nods and moves on. My thoughts immediately stray back to the enticing little bookstore owner.

Oh, I'll collect. Just not the way they meant me to.

Chapter Four

Carrie

I haven't been to the store for three days. I'm too terrified to go back. I've hidden in my shame, mortified that I never called the cops, that all I did was lock up, take Cookie with me and limp home, my mascara running down my cheeks, my bottom burning.

The Italian gangster has been on my mind day and night as the stinging has abided. I've put my hands between my legs and made up stories of how he did... more... I shouldn't fantasize about an encounter that could have been rape – what he did is already definitely assault in the eyes of the law – but I'm burning up with need, wanting those cold-hot eyes on me again, that large palm connecting with the skin on my ass, creating that delicious, perfect sting.

Oh my God, I want to feel that again. Just once more in my life. To fully give up control and... just give in.

I'm not right in the head.

'Do as you're told.'

Oh, hell no!

My insides crawl with increasing unease as the bruises fade. I can't leave the store closed. I must go in, open up, do my job, and earn a living. If he, or anyone else for that matter, returns I will contact the cops for sure. I won't pay protection money to some crook who thinks he can bully me into submission, into giving him my hard-earned income. Two hundred dollars a week? Does he have any idea how many more cupcakes I'd have to sell? Maybe selling books and cupcakes isn't rocket science, maybe it seems silly and light, but my father built this business with love, and I have given it my everything to maintain his legacy.

The scent of coffee has spread throughout the house. I started the brewer as soon as I got out of bed, before I had barely even opened my eyes, and I'm almost skipping down the steps as I head back down to the kitchen after showering. It's a little past six in the morning, and even though I'm filled with apprehension, it's also a relief to resume my old habits. I'll throw down a cup of java, go fetch Cookie, and then I have some heavy-duty baking to do. Everything came to a halt when I fled. I had to cancel deliveries and managed to get my neighbor to swing by and hang a sign on the door, saying I was ill, all while I was burning up with shame. In all these years, we were never closed. Except when Mom died. We were closed then.

I come to a full stop, my sock-clad heels skidding on the tiled floor. In the middle of my bright, sunny kitchen is a huge shadow, a looming, sinister shape that seems to suck all the light to him. The Italian gangster is standing in my kitchen, holding a cup – one of *my* cat-shaped coffee cups – calmly sipping from it. I give out a choked cry as my chest tightens in fear. I stumble back, my legs feeling like over-cooked pasta. Flailing, I fight to find the doorframe to get support, then I spin around to flee only to lose my breath as he throws his arm around my waist.

"No!"

I may have had silly daydreams of a certain scary man who wants to spank my behind, but this is real, and this man is dangerous.

"Shhh, *principessa*, no screaming, little one." His mouth is right by my ear, his voice calm, and he smells so good. There's the familiar quality of coffee, a pinch of cedar and cinnamon, with undertones of something musky, him. His words rumble in his chest, reverberating through me, forcing the last air out of my lungs.

I widen my eyes, inhaling to scream for help, for someone to come to my rescue, but before I can make a noise, he spins me around, pushes me up against the wall, and puts a finger to my lips.

"You are a naughty little girl, are you not?"

He tuts, looking me over. All I have on is a pink T-shirt with text across my chest that says 'eat me' above the image of a piece of cake, white cotton panties, and pink unicorn slippers.

I'm going to die in shame.

Or of shame.

Whichever happens first.

"What are you doing here?" I sputter, my mind finally connecting with my mouth, making me able to put together at least one sentence. I'm acutely aware of his closeness, his warmth, and his overwhelming presence in my little house. I'm all too aware of all the things I've imagined this man doing to me, and I am horrified at the idea that he'd somehow magically know.

"You are a difficult girl to find, Miss Ellerbrock. Whose house is this?" He cocks his head and glances around us before he looks back at me.

"It was my father's."

"And where is Father now?"

"He died."

"And why is your name not on the house?"

"I had to borrow money to keep Princess

running. The house is... in the name of my ex... boyfriend. He... helped me." Ethan actually came through for me even though we had broken up. It was an emergency, and even if I'm glad he helped me out, it makes me indebted to someone I'd rather not be. He has money, and he offered. It stood between accepting his help or losing both my business and my home.

He growls. Growls. "And where is the boyfriend?"

"Ex!"

"Whatever. Where?"

"He's out of the picture."

"But you live in a house with his name to it? Your father's house, but someone else owns it? I don't like this picture."

"Living in this town is expensive, dude!"

The Italian's eyes flash dangerously, and I swallow hard, immediately filing away 'dude' as a word not to use on him. "Running the store even more so. I can't pay the money you want!"

He scoffs and suddenly lets me go, taking a step back. "I don't want any money from you."

My mouth falls open. I'm not hearing this right. "But I thought... You said..."

"I don't care about money. I want something much sweeter."

A sucking sensation starts in the pit of my belly, and it grows exponentially as he lets his eyes travel down my body, past my breasts, my bare thighs, landing on the fluffy unicorn heads on my feet.

"You were hiding from me. I didn't care for it. You were hard to find. It was infuriating."

"You threatened me."

He raises a shoulder in half shrug then drops it. "It was my job."

"You hit me!"

"If I had hit you, you would be in the hospital. I spanked you for your insolence, and I will do it again, little girl, for all the time I've had to spend looking for you."

My heart hammers wildly as I look left and right, trying to find an escape. He tsks, immediately catching my attention.

"Do you like to be chased, little girl? I like a good chase."

That heady, heavy sensation that settles between my legs can't possibly be excitement, can it?

He takes a step back, still holding me pinned to the wall with his intense green gaze.

Another step.

He's baiting me. I'm not playing his games.

Another step.

He's right out of arm's reach. I look at the doorway then back to him. My heart speeds up, and my mouth turns dry like sandpaper.

Not gonna run. It's what he wants.

Another step.

He's looking for a reason to punish you, silly girl, don't fall for it.

Every instinct screams at me to run. My brain disconnects from my legs, and I throw myself toward the doorway. If I can only get out the front door, the neighbors will see me, and I'll be safe.

Chapter Five

Tommaso

The American girl dashes to the left, like a frightened bunny, a little whimper climbing out of her throat. She's playing my kind of game. I wonder if she knows it? I wonder if she's playing, too?

For the thrill of it, because I have a twisted mind that gets off on the hunt, I let her reach the front door. Before she has a chance to put her hand on the doorknob, I cover the distance and have her in my arms, lifting her away from her one shot at freedom. She inhales to scream, so I slam a hand over her generous lips, pulling her tight to my chest and tut.

"Such a naughty girl."

She squirms, then slams her head back, almost hitting my chin. She's too short, and too soft, to be a match to me, and even though I like how her squirming rubs her round ass against my cock, I also want to see that same ass blush in fierce competition with her cheeks as I slap her bottom.

"Get off me, you filthy fucking bastard! You can't just barge into my home!" She twists and turns, stomps her heel on my foot hard enough for it to hurt. "I'm calling the cops!"

Throwing herself forward, she shifts us, and I almost topple over, but regain my footing. As I'm bent over, she slams her head back again, this time hitting my nose so hard my face explodes in pain.

I groan and put a hand to my nose. It comes away bloody. I lose my hold on the little hellion, and she takes the chance to jerk free and manages to get a hand on the doorknob, twisting it. The door opens a sliver, and she almost, almost escapes. She's a clever little girl, no doubt, but I'm stronger, and have learned to ignore my discomfort when other matters are more urgent.

Stopping her is much more important than a bloody nose.

I shoot forward, wrap my arms around her waist, and yank her to me, falling on my back with the girl on top of me. The air is slammed out of my lungs, and I gasp as I twist us around until I have her pinned beneath me. There is no stopping her struggles. I need to change tactics, or I'll have to use more force than I want to. I have no intention of hurting Miss Ellerbrock. I don't know why I've been so obsessed with her, but spanking her in that office, smelling the excitement all over her, has rendered me sleepless since.

Squeezing her throat, more as a warning than to cut off her breathing, I put my mouth to her ear. *"Calm down, little one. I don't want to hurt you, girl."*

She freezes, her breaths come as short gasps. "What?"

Realizing I spoke to her in my mother tongue, I dare to free one arm and push some of the blond locks off her cheek so I can catch her gaze. Huge blue eyes stare at me, frightened. Understandably. Sadly. That's who I am, all I have ever been, the cruel enforcer.

"Come on, get up. Stop fighting me." I push up, jump to my feet, and offer her my hand.

She's still flat on her belly, eyeing my hand, and the door behind me. She moves faster than I expect, kicking out her foot, hitting my legs.

Italiano has many more colorful curses than English, and a long string of them passes my lips as I pounce on her. "You are begging for trouble!" I straddle her and push up her arms on her back, circling her wrists with one hand while I bear down the other on her delicious full ass.

Smack. "Stop." *Smack.* "Fighting." *Smack.* "Me."

She hollers and tries to get loose, but I have her now, perfectly bundled up beneath me, and I'm going nowhere. Everything about her screams of loneliness, and of the need for a firm hand. Everything about her invites me in. She is chaos. I am order. She is fiery embers. I am permafrost.

"Please! What do you want?"

"Who am I?"

"I don't know!" she hollers.

"What do you need?"

She squirms, but only manages to trap herself tighter between my thighs. My cock is unapologetically hard, twitching, weeping to be freed of its restraints. It would be so easy to put my hand between her legs, coax her ready for me, make her shake with reluctant need before I pull down her pristine white cotton panties and bury myself to the hilt in her pussy.

Her face is flushed, she's still fighting. "I need you to get off me."

"No. That's not what you need. You need some order back into your life."

"What are you talking about? Get off me! You're heavy!"

"Look at this place, Miss Ellerbrock. Look at the state you're in. Look at the mess in the kitchen." I lean in and catch her gaze, then I turn my head to look at the floor under a chair that stands before us. "And look at the size of... what do you call it? Dust bunnies? And you haven't taken care of your business for three days."

"You don't get to tell me what to do!"

I tut. The sound makes her flinch slightly. "But you are in desperate need of one who does." I slide a hand past her hip, down along the delicious curvature of her bottom, where warm skin meets my fingers. The girl trembles, holds her breath, and waits. She knows what's coming. I feel it in my bones. She waits, wants, needs, just as much as I do. I raise my arm and then bear down on her ass. She squeals.

"Aren't you?"

"No!"

I slap her again, just hard enough to sting and leave a quickly fading blush. "Tell me you will do as you're told."

"Never."

She jerks and screams, trying to get me off her. I smack her again.

"Tell me you want me to take care of you."

"No!"

My palm connects with the naked skin on her ass, a tad harder than before.

"You have no control over your business. You're on the edge of ruin. You live in a pigsty. Your father's house is owned by another man. Tell me again you don't need me."

"I—I don't need you, you—pervert!"

I remind her with a firm smack of the consequences of being mouthy with me. She gasps then grits her teeth.

"I am going to take care of you, Carrie Ellerbrock. I'm going to free you, but there will be a price."

A teardrop glitters in her lower eyelashes. I abandon her blushing behind and catch the tear on the last knuckle of my index finger.

"Who am I?"

"Get out of here!" she screams, her face turning even redder than before.

I spank her again. Harder this time. Her annoying persistence is getting to me. My nose pounds with pain, my mouth tastes of iron, and I've hated every minute of my life for the past few days. I've hated it since the moment I set my foot on American soil. I hate that I have taken on a child's job and have had to threaten this young lady. I hate that she disappeared and made my days even darker. I feared she had gone and done something stupid.

I sit down even heavier on her, squeezing her between my thighs while I tighten my hold on her wrists. Caressing her cheek, I grab her hair and force her to meet my gaze.

"I am going nowhere, and you are going to calm down. Get up." I stand and pull her with me in one move, then I march her before me back to the kitchen where I maneuver her to sit on a chair while I go to pour her a cup of coffee and refill my own kitty-cat cup.

I push the cup into her shaking hands. It irks me to see her so afraid of me. I'll make it up to her.

Somehow. Maybe I simply should have knocked? It just doesn't have the same impact on people to follow the rules of courtesy. I make my own rules.

"Drink."

She looks between me, the cup and to something behind me. I grab my own cup and take a sip, mixing the sweet taste of blood with the weak flavor of American coffee. I grimace. One of the many things I need to teach this lady: to make real coffee – the kind that makes a man's palate bounce from the shock and that can wake the dead.

"Can I have the whitener?"

I narrow my eyes. Whatever that is, I'm sure it's not something that belongs in coffee. She holds my gaze a few seconds longer, then she sighs and puts the cup to her mouth, drinking, an adorable frown forming between her eyebrows.

I grab a chair and flip it around, straddling it. Leaning my arms on the backrest, I tentatively touch my swollen nose. *Cazzo!* I hope it isn't broken.

The girl clutches the cup in her hands, her eyes following my every move. "Who are you?"

"My name is Tommaso Vittelli of the Vittelli clan. I'm one of four brothers. Together, we run an empire."

"In Italy?"

"Correct."

"Huh, so I was right." She worries her plump bottom lip with her teeth, making me want to reach out and caress away her concern. But I don't. I recognize that she needs to work through this. "Then what are you doing here? Why do you run around threatening small business owners in LA?"

I sigh. Why indeed? "My brother Stephano is hopelessly stupid. We made a deal to get him out of the mess he made."

"You're not happy about it."

"I was unhappy. Now I'm very happy."

"With the USA?"

"No, I'm very unhappy with the US. But I'm happy with my little *principessa*."

"Me?" Her face turns several shades darker. "I'm not... yours, Tommaso."

I tut and shake my head. "See, this is where you are mistaken, *tesoro*. I'm here to take care of you. I'm not asking." I give the backrest a light slap and stand. "Go get yourself dressed. I will prepare breakfast."

"I don't need—"

I stand and stare her down, putting the full force of my willpower behind my glare.

She snaps her mouth shut, then throws up her hands. "Fuck! Whatever."

"Language," I say.

She looks as if she's about to object, but then thinks better of it.

I smile. "That's my good girl."

Chapter Six

Carrie

I lurch to my feet, unsure if he'll pounce on me again. I don't want him to make me breakfast. I'd rather he keeps threatening me. I don't want someone to care for me. If I do, I'm afraid it will open the lid I've closed so carefully over my vulnerable core, over the little girl who is so hopelessly lost.

His gaze burns holes in my back as, with lead-filled legs, I drag myself up the stairs to put on more clothes. I clutch the hem of the T-shirt and try to make it cover my ass, embarrassed to hell by how my skin tingles with the memory of his hand.

I should make a run for it. I could jump out a window from the second floor, run to my neighbor and call the cops. So why do I already know I won't? He's pushing all the right buttons. Does he know it?

I have my regular customers to chat with, and a few friends scattered across the continent from my high school years. I don't have any other relatives. I'm painfully lonely, but as long as I bury myself in work, bake, read, eat, and sleep, I don't have the time to think about the years that rush by, about the life I'm losing. I'm twenty-eight years old with no children, and no man. I've begun to accept that I'll end up an old cat lady who will one day be found half eaten, dead for weeks because no one missed me. Of course, I don't have any cats. Yet. It's a work in progress.

The knowledge that he, Tommaso, is moving around in my house makes me antsy. I'm not thinking straight, and I can't focus on what to wear, knowing he's downstairs. Desperate to rectify the semi-naked situation, I quickly pull on a pair of light pink sweatpants that I find tossed on the floor next to my bed. As soon as I rip off the T-shirt with its embarrassing message, I wrestle on a bra and finally a fresh T-shirt out of the pile of unsorted clothes I haven't moved into the closet yet.

He's right. My life is a mess. How the hell does he know that? I dash down the stairs, two steps at a time, and skid to a halt before him. He has removed his suit jacket and rolled up his shirt sleeves. A towel doubles as an apron, tucked inside the waist of his pants. The muscles in his thick forearms coil as he stirs a yellow, quickly coagulating serving of scrambled eggs in my frying pan. He glances at me as I warily approach him, stops his stirring motion, and turns to me, shaking his head as he purses his lips.

"This is what you wear for work?"

I pull at the hem of the T-shirt. "What?"

He raises his eyebrows.

Oh, for fuck's sake. "Mm-no." My cheeks heat up.

"So why are you dressed like that? Go put on something nice. Take your time. Give me a few minutes and I will have prepared breakfast for you. And coffee, *tesoro*, will be served black from now on."

I put my hands on my hips. "For you, maybe. My taste buds are still alive and well and will be cared for with cream and sugar, thank you very much."

He curls his lips in distaste and sighs. "I will teach you, little *principessa*."

There's something so incredibly sexy about this man making me breakfast. I drink him in, look at those large hands, and then drop my gaze to his flaw-lessly polished shoes. What do they say about men with large hands and feet?

I choke down a groan and flee back upstairs to put on what I usually wear. Polka dots – a wide skirt and a tight blouse. Today I go for baby blue. I only slob around at home when no one sees me. Except today he has— the scary, oddly intriguing stranger who forced himself into my house, into my life.

The scent of fresh coffee, toast, and scrambled

eggs makes my mouth water as I run back down again.

"Good, here you are. Now eat. You need a good breakfast to start a busy day right." He sits with nothing but a cup of coffee in front of him. The other side of the table has a plate with toast and a slice of cheese, a second plate with the eggs, a cup of coffee and an apple next to it.

My stomach makes a loud noise as I sit in front of him, and I push a hand to my midsection, avoiding his gaze as I begin to stuff my face. I don't know how I can have an appetite in his overbearing presence, but I'm starved, and the food tastes so good. I haven't had anyone cook for me since... I can't remember when. I always looked after Dad. I took care of Ethan.

I eat and fight the tears that want to escape.

"What do you want?" I finally ask, still chewing.

"I want you to eat your breakfast."

"And then? I need to go get Cookie and then get to the shop. I need to bake."

He shrugs. "Then that's what I want you to do."

"You're confusing me."

He shrugs again. "Change of plans."

"I thought you wanted protection money?" I push in the last bite of toast and swallow it down with a too-large sip of the strong, bitter coffee he's made.

"I already told you I don't care about money, but I will protect you."

"From whom?" I narrow my eyes. "At what cost?"

"Clever girl. There is a cost, but I think you are more than willing to pay the price."

I stand so abruptly the chair topples. "Get out of here! I'm not doing anything with you."

He doesn't even flinch. "Sit."

"I have to go. I'm in a hurry."

He stands. "Then I'll drive you."

"No! I... need to walk Cookie."

"What is Cookie?"

"My neighbor's dog."

He processes this. "Very well, then I'll walk with you."

I groan. Man, he's persistent. "Let me brush my teeth. I'll be back in a sec," I mutter and make a beeline to the little bathroom behind the kitchen.

Sara, my neighbor, keeps throwing funny gazes at Tommaso, who stands like a statue on the sidewalk, observing us with his intense gaze.

"Who is that?"

Who indeed? I accept the leash and give Cookie a good rub behind her ear. "Hey, girl! He's... a friend."

Sara raises her eyebrows and appreciation glints

in her eyes. "Really? That's about time. That you got yourself some... friends, I mean."

His presence burns holes in my back during the whole exchange. I slap her lightly on her shoulder. "Shh! That's not how it is."

She studies him then looks at me again, her lips pursed. "Then that's how it should be."

"I'll be back with Cookie tonight," I mutter. "See you."

I walk down the steps with an overjoyed dog bouncing next to me. I'm hoping she'll growl at the stranger, but instead they become immediate friends. Tommaso rubs Cookie's sweet spot, and she all but rolls over for him. I groan inwardly. What is that? Some animal connection? No one is on my side, it seems.

"Let's walk, then." I mutter. I want to stomp my foot. I'm annoyed, I'm enticed, and I really want this weird man to explain himself. "You have thirty minutes. When we get there, I really need to get to work."

We walk side by side in the early morning. Cookie is all over the place, dragging me nearly off my feet, the way she always does in the morning. After a few minutes, Tommaso takes the leash out of my hands, reels it in and has Cookie trot obediently next to him as if it's the easiest thing in the world.

"It's very simple. I will take care of you for the rest of my stay here."

"I don't need to be taken care of," I snap.

But I'm lying. I don't know this man. All I know is that he's probably dangerous. Still, he evokes a longing in me, and every time he says the magic words 'take care of', my stomach flips with the need to fall to my knees and beg him to do it.

"We both know that is a lie, Miss Ellerbrock. Do yourself a favor and don't ever try to lie to me again. Lies carry consequences." His deep voice with that harsh accent, delivering the admonishing words, makes my insides hot and squirmy.

"How... How long is your stay here?"

"Six months. Six months that I thought were going to be hell on earth, but I just found a way to make them much more... pleasurable."

Chapter Seven

Carrie

Ohhh, that heat inside me – it just exploded into a volcanic eruption of epic proportions.

"Me?" Why does my voice come out as a puny squeak?

"Yes, Miss Ellerbrock," he says with the slightly impatient tone of a teacher whose favorite student has yet again failed an assignment. "You."

"But... what do you want from me?"

"You will do what I tell you, when I tell you. I will reward you when you're being a good girl, and I will punish you when you disobey me."

"Punish?" I sputter.

"Acknowledging is the first step to acceptance."

Aaahhh! "I didn't mean—"

He tuts and holds up a hand. "You're on the plus

side right now. Make sure to stay there. You might not like my punishments."

My butt vividly remembers his large palm connecting with it. Over and over. The memory makes my pussy burn. I don't know if the spankings count as reward or as punishment, and I'm loath to ask, so I press my lips together and keep walking.

"So... six months? Then you'll leave?"

"I'll leave the city, the country, the whole western hemisphere. You will never see me again."

Why doesn't that feel as good as it should? Damn.

"And you want to 'take care' of me until then? That sounds pretty fucking ominous."

"No cursing, Miss Ellerbrock. I dislike those words from your pretty lips."

"I'll say whatever the fuck I want."

He stops so abruptly, grabbing my arm, and pushing me up against the brick wall of the house we're passing, that my mind spins from disorientation. "No. You will not. You will say and do exactly what I tell you from now on," he growls.

"I'm not selling my body to you!" I snap.

"Good," he says, "I wasn't looking for a whore."

"I'm not a fucking whore!"

"You have a foul mouth, *tesoro*. We will work on that."

I try to dodge him and get out from between his heavy body and the brick wall, but it's as if I'm trapped between two rocks. Cookie paces nervously, looking between the two crazy humans, clearly in conflict with herself and needing to defend someone, but she can't figure out who. Cookie, me! Chew on his leg! But she settles for a whiny noise and then a bark aimed at us both. I read it loud and clear: 'Behave, you silly humans. I want to munch on my favorite bone, I want my bowl of water and to try to get inside your bakery. Stop fighting.'

I force myself to relax. The heat is rising steadily as the sun climbs the sky. Little beads of sweat curl the hair at the Italian gangster's temples. His cheeks are flushed, but the corners of his mouth are turned up in amusement. He is annoyingly composed while I fight the scream that wants out.

"Are you gonna be in my hair all day?"

He raises his gaze to my hair, then looks back at me, his eyes twinkling. "No, *principessa*. I will put your tiara in place, then I'll be on my way. I have plenty of things to do with my days."

"Threatening other shop owners?" I spit.

He cocks his head and gives a half-shrug. "Among other things."

"I should call the cops."

"Then why haven't you? What has stopped you?"

"You... slamming me against a wall."

"And after that?"

I clench my jaw and look away, too embarrassed to meet his gaze. What indeed?

He smiles and squares his shoulders while tucking a lock of hair behind my ear. "I know why you haven't called the cops."

I try to choke down the gasp. He can't know of the rush that shoots through me when he touches me like that, about the depths of my need for someone to see me, to want me, to care for me, for once.

I put my hands on my hips. "Yeah? And why is that?"

He leans in. I have nowhere to go.

Closer. A breath away.

"Because you want more."

I inhale to object, because it's in my nature to do so, but he steals my thoughts, then my mind, my will, and finally my breath, as he presses his lips against mine in a kiss that is over all too soon.

"Come, Miss Ellerbrock. You will be late." He takes my hand and places it in the crook of his arm, and then we walk.

Or he walks. I stumble after him, dazed. He swamps my senses: the taste of Italian gangster on my lips, his spicy scent in my nose, the muscles in his arm coiling beneath my fingers. I want to sniff him all over and fill my lungs with that edible scent, but I lift my chin and keep my nose to myself. I want to squeeze and see what he feels like, if he's made of stone or flesh, but I force my touch to remain light.

He follows me inside, making a lap around the kitchen, his hands behind his back, as if he's inspecting his new domain. After looking through the rooms in the basement, he disappears upstairs for a while. I make Cookie comfortable, then I get to work, preparing dough, the whole time acutely aware of his existence somewhere in the vicinity.

"I will come to pick you up after work. Do you close at six? Do you always walk?"

I almost jump through the roof, my heart shooting to my throat. "Fuck!"

Tommaso holds up my tiara and puts a hand on my shoulder, turning me toward him. He tuts as he strokes hair off my face and then carefully puts the jewelry in place. "Such a foul mouth on such a pretty girl. I told you no swearing. Tonight, you will receive ten slaps for your disobedience. Say 'yes, I understand, thank you for your care'."

I stare at him, speechless. My mouth falls open, but no words come out. He waits. For me. To be coherent.

"Carrie. With every second you wait with your answer, I will add a slap. I can be patient, but this is tiring."

"Yes, I understand!" I blurt out.

Hot and cold runs along my back. The chill makes my heart tremble while the heat settles between my legs. What the hell did I just agree to?

A beautiful smile spreads across his face. "Good girl. I will work on your reward."

I gasp and widen my eyes. "Reward?"

His smile turns into a smirk. "After you have taken your punishment."

The pathetic mewl that climbs up my throat makes my cheek burn in fierce competition with my pussy.

Carrie

My Italian gangster sits in one of the armchairs. One moment he isn't there, the next he is. I never heard the bell of the front door. How the hell did he sneak in so quietly?

"Miss Ellerbrock. Have you had a good day?"

"It's been... interesting." I put a hand over my heart, willing it to calm down.

He stands and stalks toward me. "How so?"

I fight the instinct to back away. "Just... been thinking."

"Have you now? And what have you been thinking about?"

My cheeks heat up, and I know I'm blushing furiously. "Stuff," I mumble and turn to flee. I don't know where to, though. Tommaso Vittelli has inserted himself into my life, and somehow, I've let him. His hand clamps around my wrist, preventing me from escaping.

"What 'stuff'?"

His voice is warm and rough at the same time, with dangerous edges and an alluring purr. It does funny things to my private parts.

"Like who you've been threatening today."

"So, you've been thinking about me, then?" He sounds pleased, and how can I deny that? He's been on my mind 24/7 since I first saw him.

His touch burns my flesh, his closeness seems to steal the air in the room. "I... need to lock up," I whisper.

"Then by all means, do it."

"You're holding me."

He's so close, almost chest to chest, towering over me, wrapping me in his demanding presence and enticing scent. Every detail of his tailored suit jacket, the dark gray tie in a discreet rhomboid pattern, the top button of his shirt visible where the tie hangs slightly askew, stands out unnaturally clear, like in a fever dream. Without warning, he lets me go and holds out his hand in a gesture for me to pass him. I twitch into action and hurry to complete the closing procedures, locking the double locks, pulling down the security bars, putting today's measly earnings in a bag for later deposit at the bank, and stuffing it in the safe. All the while, I'm acutely aware of Tommaso, studying my every move.

When I'm done, he approaches me and raises his arms. I fight to not flinch. I never know what he's up to, and his promise of a punishment has remained at the forefront of my mind the whole day. All he does, though, is to carefully untangle the tiara from my hair and tuck some loose strands behind my ear.

"Time to go," he says.

I follow him mindlessly, like a faithful dog, through the store, past my office where he neatly places the tiara on the desk.

My neighbor looks like a cat with a bowl of cream when we return Cookie, her gaze darting between me and Tommaso.

"Not a word," I tell her.

"About damn time," she retorts. "He looks like someone who would take care of you, and God knows you'd need it.

"Tomorrow," I mutter, and leave.

"What did the two of you talk about?" asks Tommaso when we begin the last leg of the walk before we're at my house.

"Stupid things."

"Indulge an old man."

"None. Of. Your. Business. And you're not that old."

"When we get inside, I want you to pull your pants down and bend over my knee."

"What? No!"

"This is what you agreed to. You need discipline. I will provide it."

"No!" My heart speeds up almost impossibly, thrashing inside my rib cage. "I don't need you spanking me!"

"Well... suck it up, my *principessa*. This is happening. You can panic, or you can be rational about it."

I'm not rational about it. It's as if a volcano has erupted in the pit of my belly, and lava spreads to my pussy, making it spasm with heat. My mind tells me to run, but my brain has left the building, and I'm nothing but a flurry of hormones, riding the heatwave that both the Californian summer and the Italian's appearance in my life has created.

In my hallway stand three pitch black suitcases, all the same size, neatly placed with the same distance between them. I stop so abruptly Tommaso walks right into me. I stare at the three menacing-looking items, knowing full well what I'm seeing, and at the same time unable to take in the turn of events. Then I spin to face the infuriating gangster.

"You're not moving in here!" Then it dawns on me. "Do you have my keys?"

He doesn't even blink at my outburst as he

removes his suit jacket, puts it on a hanger, then closes the door to the outside world.

"I had a copy made for myself, and of course I am. Now, you can either go peacefully, or I can throw you over my shoulder and carry you into the living room, but you're going, either way."

"You're kidding me!" I try to detect any sign that he's just joking, a humorous glint in those clear green eyes, a little twitch in the corner of his mouth, partly hidden by the beard, but he looks dead serious, and my stomach plummets.

"I'm not. I will not hesitate to use force, but it's better if you learn to submit, little one. Thirteen slaps on your naked butt for your repeated use of curse words this morning."

"Fuck you!" I snarl and try to dart to the side to get past him. But he's faster. Much faster. The next moment he has me pinned against the wall, his body covering mine, his delicious, terrifying hard planes meeting my soft flesh. I've never felt so vulnerable, so naked, before in my life.

"Miss Ellerbrock." His lips move against my ear, the beard tickling my skin, and I go still in fearful and ridiculously aroused expectation of what's to follow. "I never back down. I can't be bargained with. I punish people for a living. You will not be able to talk your way out of this, and you cannot run. Thirteen slaps on your bare behind. The last curse you used goes on tomorrow's tally. Thirteen slaps, then I will reward you for brightening my day with your mere existence. Now, say 'thank you', and do as I tell you."

I want to fight it, I really do. I'm a modern woman. I don't need to be taken care of. I'm not supposed to be punished like some Victorian school-child, but everything he says strikes a chord in me. I long for a clearer path, for some order, and for someone to manage me the way I've always dreamt of. My tongue forms the words, over and over. I'm not fighting him so much as I'm fighting myself. My whole resistance drains out of me, and I sag in his hold, giving in, fully and completely.

"Thank you, Tommaso."

He smiles beautifully, making my heart somersault. "That's my good girl."

Chapter Nine

Tommaso

Her eyes are glazed as she pulls up her skirt to her waist, pushes down her panties, and with hesitant, jerky moves, bends over my lap. She takes her time, draping herself across my thighs, her body tense like a piano wire. I let her fight herself, and when she's finally settled into an awkward position, I grab her hips and pull her to me, arranging her the way I want her. My cock strains my pants, and I want to do so much more than just make the skin of her ass sting, but I'm a man of honor. Somewhat. This session is about punishment, and to train her to submit to my will.

I'll fuck her later.

I will teach her my preferences, learn all about

what she likes, explore every inch of her voluptuous body, and make her weep with need for me.

Carrie Ellerbrock is a one-of-a-kind woman, an unexpected find in this suburban hellhole, an uncut diamond that I plan to polish into a shining gem.

"Such a good girl," I coo as I stroke my palm across her pale ass, bared for me. She trembles, and her chest heaves with every breath. I don't think it's only fear. I don't even think it's mostly fear. When I spanked her back in her office that first day, the scent of her arousal hit me like a sledgehammer. She wants this badly but has never dared to ask for it.

"Panna cotta, Carrie, is your safeword. You know what it's used for? Repeat it."

"Mm-hmm." She exhales in short gasps. "Panna cotta? I'll never remember that. Why?"

"It's my favorite dessert. It's what I think of when I think of you. Do you want something else?"

She's silent a few moments. "Okay. Panna cotta."

"Good girl," I whisper.

My arm raised, I bear down on her right ass cheek. Hard. She jerks and gasps. I wait for her to settle, then I repeat the slap on the left side. A groan escapes her, but she doesn't fight me, doesn't try to get up.

"Count for me, *principessa*. Count and remember why this is happening."

"Bastard," she grits out.

I tut.

"Two," she adds in a rush.

I bring my hand down again. Right, left, right, left, waiting for her count. The words are gasped with increasing strain. Her skin blooms red, warm, no doubt stinging. Beautiful.

"Thirteen," she finally squeals. "Ow!"

"Such an uneven number," I say teasingly.

"No! It's enough! I'll be good."

I smile as I caress her reddened skin, making her shudder. I wait. She should know what to do.

"I'll be good, I promise. Th-thank you."

My smile broadens into a grin. My balls ache, and I'm fighting my inner beast hard, pushing him down. I want to fuck her so badly, but it will have to wait. She deserves her reward.

"Good, good girl. Now get up and come with me."

She lurches to her feet, her face as flushed as her bottom, her blond locks in disarray. She makes a move to pull up her panties, then hesitates, looking at me for confirmation. I nod, ridiculously pleased with her obedience.

"Upstairs bathroom," I say. "After you."

I haven't only been dishing out cruelty for the local gang of not-so-organized crime today. I have made some other arrangements, too.

She stops in the doorway, and her pretty mouth falls open, then she turns to me, her big blue eyes wide and confused. "When— What did you—"

I shrug, feigning indifference, but I'm pleased with myself. I had someone come by and install a clawfoot bathtub. I've also cleaned up her mess of laundry, half-empty bottles, and used Q-tips; positioned some scented candles on a shelf; and bought her new towels. It is a minor effort that has worked wonders. I like a home tidy, and I'm no stranger to pulling up my sleeves and doing whatever is needed. Today, she needed this. She's been forced to deal with me, and I'm no breeze. I want to show her that she can also relax, that good can come out of this, too.

"Did you do this?"

I nod.

"For me?"

I tilt my head again in acknowledgement.

"Oh. My. God. I love it."

I move past her, pick up the lighter I left in one of the drawers, and light the candles. A scent of jasmine soon surrounds us, and the yellow light flickers invitingly, reflected in the white-tiled walls.

"I will be downstairs. Take a bath, relax. This is your reward. I can both give and take. This is me giving. If you keep on being my good girl, there will be more rewards in the future. I keep my promises. Dinner will be ready in about forty minutes."

Her mouth is still open in surprise. "Oh... okay. Wow."

"What do you say?"

The answer comes immediately, her cheeks flushing furiously. "Thank you."

I must leave while I still can. Almost doubled over from need, I make my way to the kitchen and hear the water run upstairs.

I wanted to make her an Italian meal for our first dinner, and I have already prepared it. It's a deceivingly simple risotto, but there is nothing simple about the dish. The creamy rice gets its golden color from saffron, and sometimes it's called risotto *allo zafferano*. Arborio rice is cooked with veal broth, butter, and Grana Padano cheese.

The secret to making a great risotto *alla Milanese* lies in giving the rice time to absorb the flavors. I told her forty minutes. It will be enough time for us both. I want her to come back down soft, unafraid, and ready. I have had fearful people all around me for as long as I can remember. I don't want Miss Ellerbrock to be afraid. I want her to want me.

The realization makes me stagger, and I must sit as I struggle with the implications. I'm a loner. It's the only thing I know. My family is a fucked-up mess. My life is violence. Finding myself on the other side of the hemisphere, alone and frustrated, has screwed up my bearings more than I thought. What am I doing here? What makes me want to toy with this young woman? What possessed me to bare her ass and force myself on her the way I did? Everything about her pulls me in. Her eyes plead with the natural protector in me, her full curves make the predator I hide throw himself at the bars of his cage. My veneer of civility is thin, and being around her has already made it crack in several places.

The table is set. Everything is ready. Except I'm not. I stand, with half a mind to go grab my suitcases and get the hell out of here when she suddenly stands in the doorway.

Soft, a flowery scent accompanying her, a short white dress hugging her hips and breasts.

Demure, yet proud and unafraid.

Everything I ever wanted.

I can stay.

It's only for a few months, anyway.

I smile, and something in my chest swells. A bar in that cage breaks. It's the first, and I fear it won't be the last. My beast roars in delight.

"Welcome. Please, have a seat."

Chapter Ten

Tommaso

I sleep in her guest room, eat breakfast and dinner at her table, walk her and the dog to and from work, deliver delicious spankings when needed – every day it turns out – but I make no move to touch her sexually.

And it's killing us both.

Death can be slow and sweet, packaged in pink and gold, shaped like a woman.

Everything inside me is wrapped up in tightly coiled knots, but between the two of us, I believe that young Miss Ellerbrock is worse off. At least I can take out some of my frustration at work.

Her eyes follow me wherever I go, and she has stopped trying to hide that she's staring. She consumes me with her gaze, and as the heat rises outdoors to unbearable levels, a tropical storm rises inside that no air conditioner can manage.

Her skirt is up, her white cotton panties pulled down to right where her deliciously rounded ass cheeks meet her thighs. The musk wafting up from between her legs is maddening.

"I've been bad, Tommaso," she says. "I was supposed to work on the accounting, but it was too hot, and the air conditioner needs fixing. It distracted me." Little beads of sweat dampen her hair and make it curl like a blond halo along the hairline of her forehead, at her temples, and in her neck. It looks absolutely adorable.

I hide my smile. I know what she really wants. She knows that I know.

But I want to hear it. I want words sweeter than sugar to spill from her lips: 'stop teasing me, touch me, fuck me, please.'

"I like how you say my name, *principessa*. It sounds funny."

"Tommaaaaaso."

I turn her away and push her flush against the dinner table, raising my hand.

Swat.

"Hey! I—"

Swat.

"Ow!"

Swat.

"Stop!"

Swat.

"Owww!" she cries! "Stop, please!"

My insides heat up, along with her delicious whimpers. Something in me grows warmer with each passing day, opens up to her, wants more, wants to let her in.

"That's my good, good girl."

"Ow." She squirms and clenches her slightly flushed ass cheeks.

I drag the tips of my fingers across her heated skin, then I blow on it lightly. "Let me make it better, *tesoro.*"

"Please." Her voice is hoarse and full of emotion, shooting a flood of need my way. I steel myself.

"Please what?"

"Please..."

"Please what?"

She is quiet. I don't think she's even breathing. I sure as hell am not.

"Please what?" I say again, so quietly I almost don't know if I spoke at all.

"Please... touch me," she finally says, in nothing more than a whisper.

But I heard. I'm so attuned to her I've heard it for a long time. I let my palm rest on her flaming skin, then caress her butt down to where the tips of my fingers meet her panties. Catching them, I stroke downward, sliding them down her smooth thighs until gravity makes them fall to her feet, where I lift one foot at a time and free her of the garment.

Carrie gasps and juts out her ass for me. So precious. So needy. Ripe for the picking. I change direction and stroke up along the inside of her thigh, almost all the way to her pussy, stopping close enough to feel the warmth, then I kick her legs further apart and push my fingers inside her in one move, reveling in her tight heat that clenches around me.

"Oh God, Tommaso," she gasps.

I slap her once, then thrust harder, in and out.

"Again," she cries. "Please."

I ache with the need to pull out my cock and bury it in her delicious pussy, but she's never gonna have to plead with me twice to slap her ass. Fucking her with my fingers, I slap her again.

"What did you call me?"

"Tommaaa—"

Slap. She's absolutely soaked and rocks her hips back against my every push.

"Try again." *Slap.*

She gets wetter each time my palm connects with her butt.

"Toooomm—"

Slap. She's such a little brat, my girl.

"You know what to call me, Carrie."

"Tooo—"

Slap.

"You're only making it worse."

Slap.

I never met anyone who loved getting spanked so much. My palm burns. Her skin is deep red and mottled. I don't know how she can take my force. I'm not even sure I'm holding back any longer.

"Tommaso, please again!"

My fingers piston in her, and I let her have it, my hand bearing down on her butt over and over.

"God!" Carrie screams and thrashes before me as her pussy walls spasm around my fingers.

She's sobbing loudly when I pull out my hand from her still-quivering flesh, pull open my pants and free my cock. I've never been so desperate to fuck someone before in my life. Sex has been nothing but a temporary release of tensions.

This – this isn't sex. I want to merge with my *principessa*. I want to fill her, take her, make her mine, and keep her.

Always.

Chapter Eleven

Carrie

I'm nowhere near done. My body hums with an orgasm that was much more than just some friction of my nethers. It feels as if he's peeled off my skin, torn the flesh off my bones, and made a Lego out of me. I need him to put me back together. I need more. More Tommaso. Much, much more.

"Please!" My voice doesn't sound like my own.

When the sound of his belt rattles, then a zipper, I thank whatever gods there might be who look out for a crazed, sex-deprived bookstore girl.

"You have been a bad girl, Carrie, begging me to hurt you, looking at me with those big, blue, innocent eyes."

I flinch when I feel his hand on my hip, but he

doesn't spank me, only grabs hold, tight. My insides weep for more.

"I'm on the pill," I whisper, my voice barely carrying the words.

"I know, *tesoro*, I live with you. I see everything."

My legs shake. I clutch the sides of the table and close my eyes. "I'll be good." I almost weep with need. "I'll be good."

He moves something between my legs, a thick hard length, strokes it up along my aching slit. I push back, wanting that something in me. Now.

"No, you won't. I don't think you will ever learn to always be good, *principessa*. But I promise to be there to guide you, and teach you, and punish you when you fail. When you fall, I will pick you up."

In one stroke, he slams inside me, filling me, stretching me, hitting my bottom, forcing all air out of my lungs from the impact. I gasp and choke, my knuckles whiten as I grip the table hard and hold on for dear life.

"Oh, you're tight," he groans.

"You're big," I pant.

"And you just—" He pulls back and then slams back inside, impaling me, "took all of me like the good, pain-loving girl you are."

My pussy clenches around his cock. His words set me ablaze again. Yes. I love pain. His pain. Only his. I love his touch. I love his soft growls and his stern ways. I love how he saw my need and forced his way into my life. I love how we are from two different worlds and still can become one so flawlessly, like peas in a pod, like a jigsaw puzzle.

Tommaso pushes up my blouse and bra. Sneaking his hand between the table and my body, he finds my nipples, twisting them, torturing them into tight buds, he makes me ache in all the right ways.

"More," I gasp. "Please."

His growl sends a shiver running down my spine, and I swear his cock grows even thicker. Until Tommaso, I didn't know I loved spanking, I didn't know I needed harsh punishments before my rewards. I know he sees me as a woman, fully and completely, but I also know he wants to be my caretaker, my man, my everything, for the duration of his stay here.

Then we'll part.

But I won't think of that just yet. We still have some months to go.

He pulls out, and I want to cry with frustration. I stagger on the verge of a second release, and he pulls out. Cruel! Unfair.

"Turn over." He grunts. "I want to see my girl."

I scramble to lie on my back, wondering if I can ever have dinner at this table again. Tommaso stands before me like a dark god, his huge cock jutting out, glistening with my juices. His normally light eyes seem to have turned black with ravenous hunger. For me. He holds my gaze and flicks open the top buttons in his shirt, then pulls it over his head and drops it to the floor. I hurry to pull off my blouse and bra that already sit askew. His chest heaves and his nostrils flare as he looks me over. I'm suddenly self-conscious. I have a few pounds extra. More than a few. More like ten. Or twenty. I'm not a pretty, skinny little model. He's probably used to those.

"Don't hide yourself from me," he snaps.

"I wasn—" I clutch my hand into a fist and force my arm back to my side. I tried to cover myself without even thinking about it.

"You are beautiful, my *principessa*. I will taste every inch of you. I will fill you with my seed. I will make you forget you ever had a life before me." He leans in, pushes I don't know how many fingers inside me, while he catches a nipple between his teeth. I draw a hissing breath, half with pleasure, half with fear.

Kissing and licking a path across my chest, his beard tickling deliciously, to the other nipple, then up my throat, he keeps talking while he thrusts his fingers in my pussy, making me arch with the rising tension and the increasing desperate need for release.

"I will punish you, and I will reward you. I own you now. No one else will ever touch my *tesoro. Non devi essere mai da sola, o spaventata, o sentirti smarrita. Sono qui adesso.*"

Oh. My. God. He mumbles words against my skin. I don't understand half of the things he's saying since he's turned to his mother tongue, but the possessive tone, his handling of my body, strumming it, playing it, making me sing a tune never heard before, makes me want to go along with anything and everything he says and does.

"I'm yours! Please."

I'm so close. I'm so, so close that I think I'll die if he doesn't let me come this instant.

His face hovers over mine, and our eyes lock. His strikingly green eyes hypnotize me, then he becomes a blur as he moves in, pressing his lips against mine, coaxing my mouth open, stealing my breath and sanity in a brutal kiss.

"I know," he mumbles into my mouth. "I know, *bella*."

After two more mind-blowing, soul-splitting orgasms – after we've fucked not only on the table, but on the kitchen floor, up against the wall in the hallway, on the sofa in the living room, after he's fucked me raw, leaving me with bruises and barely able to walk – we finally rest, sated, exhausted.

"That was—" I say.

"Intense," he fills in.

"I don't think I can move again. Ever."

He hugs me closer and presses his lips against my temple. He's drenched in sweat, and our bodies are glued together. "Are you hungry, little one?

Thirsty? Let me go fetch you something. I bought lemonade. I will bring us some. Don't move, *tesoro*."

My heart swells, bursts open. For my Italian gangster. He cares for me like no one ever has.

After kissing my temple, he then gets up with amazing vigor despite his size, and despite that he must be exhausted. It's night. We've fucked for hours. Like in the books I love to read, when two soulmates crash into each other, and nothing can hold them back. Three weeks of pent-up frustration sure took its toll. I admire his delectable ass as he leaves the room, then I fall on my back with a loud groan. I feel... complete. I feel like I won't need anything ever again. If I die tomorrow, I'll have no regrets.

A tall glass comes into my vision, its outsides already damp from condensation. The contents are white and semi-opaque, and ice cubes rattle against each other. I shoot up and grab it with greedy hands, gulping down several large swallows of the tart-sweet drink.

"Thank you."

Tommaso sits beside me, comfortable in his nudity. Like so many times before, I steal glances at his intricate tattoos. They cover parts of his chest, there are several on his arms, a couple on his knees and back. They look like nothing I've seen before. Symbols, he explained once. Each one has a meaning.

It hammered home what I already knew but hadn't wanted to think about.

Tommaso Vittelli is Italian mafia.

It's scary. It's enticing. It shouldn't make me want to crawl up in his lap and beg him to take me again. It shouldn't make me feel so safe. But he is safe. To me. In the few short weeks since he moved in, he's become my everything. I know I avoid thinking about what he does, because it would seriously screw with my sense of morality if I knew more.

"One of my father's best friends, occasionally a competitor, lives here in the US of A."

"Really? Where? What does he do?"

He gives me a deadpan look.

"Oh."

"He lives in San Francisco."

"That's not far. Did you visit?"

"Of course. He is close as family. Family is everything. He lives a good life."

"Does he have a wife? Children?"

"Luciano was always married to his work, but recently I have heard of a woman in his life."

Work. I put the glass against my cheek, trying to cool off, suddenly less at ease. "I don't think I should ask more."

"Correct, little one. You should not."

"Am I safe?"

"Safe?"

"From... your work? When you came, you asked for protection money. Protection from whom? Will your 'work' ever come visit me again?"

His eyebrows knit together into a frown, then he smiles that smile that makes my heart stutter. "I've taken care of it. You will always be safe with me."

I nod. I believe him. I don't know everything, and I won't ever want to know everything, but Tommaso is so capable. He will keep me away from any danger.

He strokes along my jawline, tucks some stray hair behind my ear, then leans in and gives me a quick kiss with lips cool from his drink. "Your house is yours again. I took care of it."

It takes me a moment, then I recoil and dart up, staring at him, my heart slamming in my chest. "What? You took care of what?"

He laughs. "Easy, easy. I paid off your loan. The dog is all right. I couldn't live in a house with another man's name on it."

"Ethan? Did you hurt *Ethan*?"

"I told you he's well. Sit down. If I hear his name on your lips again, I might consider going back. I don't like you to speak of any man besides me and your late father. Ever."

The dog. Oh. My mind spins. For a horrifying moment I thought Tommaso had gone and killed him.

"You... I..." I try to recover from the instantaneous shock of thinking Tommaso had hurt Ethan. Not that I ever want to speak to my ex again, but I wouldn't want him dead. "So now I'll live indebted to you instead?"

"Until I leave, *principessa*. Until I leave. Then you will have your life back."

Four months.

He's going back to Italy in about four months. That's when his family's debt is paid off.

Why doesn't that feel as good as it should?

"Or you could come with me, *tesoro*."

Chapter Twelve

Carrie

'Or you could come with me, *tesoro*.'

He calls me 'my love', says I'm his, wants me to leave everything behind and go with him to Italy.

Italy!

I've been out of state once in my life. That's it. I have everything here. What about my store? Who'll care for Cookie?

As weeks turn to months, our relationship settles into a new normal. Tommaso is sexually insatiable. He is always ready to go, it seems. It's dirty. It's hot. It makes me feel female on a primal level I have never experienced before. He worships my curves, makes me feel attractive and wanted, proud to be just me.

We have worked through my house and then my store at a relentless pace, throwing out or donating things I don't use, sorting everything, replacing rickety doorknobs and loose hinges.

Tommaso likes order.

I kinda like… to be ordered around.

I'll even admit I like to make a mess, and then be forced to count as he disciplines me for my messiness.

In the early evenings, right after work, he's often closed off, and a dark cloud hangs over him. In those moments, he likes it when I take over, taking care of him instead of him taking care of me.

I caress his thick, dark hair, comb my fingers through his beard. He's lying on the sofa, his head on my lap. He's even more beautiful now than the day I first met him. I have feelings. I can't hold back any longer, and knowing this will end, hurts more with each passing day.

"Tell me something about your home."

He closes his eyes, wistfulness passing across his face. He misses it.

"Milan can get hot, not like here, but the humidity is merciless. It's beautiful. There are mountains, green valleys, buildings so old you Americans could never imagine. The cafés are flooded with people, and everyone relaxes, drinks coffee, and talks about important things."

"Strong coffee?"

A fleeting smile flits on his lips. "Oh yes."

"What important things?"

"Politics. State of the world. Work…"

"Isn't that dangerous? Isn't your home like... mafia land? Can you talk about... work out in the open?"

"You need to know your friends. People get murdered for their allegiances. That's what I like about my home. It's honest."

"It sounds so different from here."

He sits up and pushes his fingers through his hair, looking like he just woke. "Do you think it's so different in the USA?"

I frown. "We're a free country, a democracy. There's a structure here that makes sense."

Tommaso barks out a loud laugh that makes me jump. "You Americans... You are so gullible. You are made to believe you live in the greatest country when in fact your organized crime is inundated in your very society."

"That's not true."

"Oh, but it is. Trust me, *bella*."

"So, tell me," I say. "What do we believe that's wrong?"

His eyebrows shoot up on his forehead. "You want to talk about politics?"

"What? Did you think I was just some dumb blonde?"

His features lighten, and I know I've reached past whatever he brought home tonight. The rest of the night he'll be funny, talk about his crazy brothers, or American soap operas, or his favorite books. He strokes my cheek, along my throat, brushes my nipple, and then pinches it into a tight little bud. Arrows of desire shoot from where he touches me to between my legs, and I automatically part my thighs for him.

"I do not think you're some dumb blonde." He pinches my nipple harder, making me gasp. "I do think you have needs, though. I think you need Tommaso to be a little rough tonight." He moves, pulls me under him, and pushes his hand inside my panties.

My only answer is an unintelligible moan.

He will take my body and make me his. Over and over until there is nothing but slick, warm skin and sated souls.

One day, a strange man stands in my kitchen. It's Sunday, and my shop is closed. Tommaso is away. He left early in the morning.

I immediately see the resemblance to my bossy Italian, but my first impression is that this man is hideous. Half his face is covered in horrible burn marks. His eyes are hard where Tommaso's are warm. He's tall and hulking.

Fear nips at my insides. Am I in danger? It feels that way.

"Hi?" My voice is unsteady. "Can I help you?"

He gives me a slow once-over, making my skin

shrink under his scrutiny, then he curls his lip. "I'm looking for Tommaso Vittelli."

"He's not here. How did you get in? Are you Stephano Vittelli?" It feels as if my life hangs on his answer." I ask because of the resemblances. I pray I'm right.

"I am. You are Miss Ellerbrock?"

I release a breath in relief. He might be dangerous, but Tommaso would have his head if he hurt me. "I am," I say, mimicking his short cut answers.

"When can I expect him?"

I shrug. "He comes and goes. Did you agree on anything? Does he know you're here?"

Stephano shakes his head. "I need to speak with him. It's urgent."

He has the same kind of polite, correct English I've grown used to from Tommaso, but he doesn't have the same heavy Italian accent.

"I can text him. Can I offer you coffee?"

"American?" He spits out the word.

"Real coffee."

I have learned. I've even learned to appreciate it.

He nods approvingly, and a small smile ghosts past his features. I see then how he is rather beautiful beneath the grim exterior. What happened to him?

I find my phone and send off a text to Tommaso.

Your brother is here. Please
hurry home

He doesn't like me bothering him while he works, but this is no small thing.

He answers almost immediately.

On my way. Be hospitable, tesoro.

Hospitable. I'm scared out of my mind.

Carrie

I hold up the phone to show Stephano the messages, then scurry to make the coffee, acutely aware of his dominating presence.

Cup placed before him, my hand shakes as I pour the hot contents. He puts his hand on mine, large and strong, to steady it.

"Why so afraid, little one?"

It's Tommaso's words from his brother's mouth. I almost swoon, despite the inner turmoil. They seem so alike.

"I'm not—"

"Is it because of my appearance?"

I half shake, half nod my head. "It's because I know who your family is," I whisper.

"Sit." His tone leaves no room for disobedience.

I sit.

He stands. Putting a cup before me, he then pours me coffee, watching me intently as I blow it and sip it with care. When I—the presumably coffee-ignorant American—don't grimace, he nods approvingly.

"I am no different from my brother. Are you afraid of him?"

"I was."

"And now?"

I shake my head.

"Then sit with me. I need someone who doesn't tremble or turn their head when they see me."

I nod, then drink again. I try to make small talk, but it's obvious Stephano is done with socializing. We sit in silence, less and less awkward, both our stances relaxing slightly. The front door slams. I shoot to my feet to greet my own tall, intimidating Italian.

He steps into the kitchen, taking over the room, my heart and my every fiber. Wrapping an arm around my shoulders, he kisses my forehead as he greets his brother.

"Stephano."

Stephano gets to his feet. "Tommaso."

"Carrie, *tesoro*, we need our privacy."

I twitch. "Of course. Anything you need?"

Tommaso shoots me a smile that—as always—makes my knees weak, a slight tension at the corners of his mouth. "You can take a bath, *bella*. I will be with you later."

I leave, stomp up the stairs a few steps, then sneak back down and put my ear to the door. My heart pounds for fear of getting discovered, but this is my first peak of anything that is Tommaso's life before I met him and nothing, not even the possible punishment for my disobedience, can pull me away from the door.

I strain to discern words in the deep voices that reverberate in my kitchen. They're alike, but with the slight edge to Stephano's voice, a darkness I'm glad Tommaso doesn't possess, and with my man's heavier, very sexy Italian accent, I still manage.

And they speak Italian. Crap.

"I prefer English." Stephano's voice.

Yes!

"*Vaffanculo*!" I recognize the curse. Then a long string of Italian.

"Tommaso," I whisper, "English."

"Fuck, all right. What are you doing in my kitchen, *fratellino*?"

I recognize this, too. The insult in 'little brother'.

And hey, *your* kitchen?

"I'm in trouble," says the brother.

"I fucking know. I'm sacrificing everything to clean your mess up."

The audacity! He doesn't like it here? With me?

My heart drops. Have I given my heart only to get it ripped out?

"You don't seem to suffer that much."

Tommaso is silent. Then: "I found something worth everything. True."

Tears well up in my eyes, and my heart resumes its right spot. Me, too. I did, too!

"But that's not it," says Stephano.

My man groans. "What else?"

"I just need advice."

"What about," spits Tommaso.

"It's a woman. An amazing woman. I've never met anyone like her, and I don't know what to fucking do."

"You? A girl?"

"She's mafia."

"What. The. Fuck? Only you. Only you, Stephano."

It's silent. For a long while. I hear chairs scrape against the floor, water flushing and the slight sloshing from the coffee brewer.

"Tell me more."

"She's the younger sister of Nathan and Christian Russo."

Silence again.

A long string of curses. These I don't recognize, but the tone of Tommaso's voice leaves no room for interpretation.

"I'm taking you home to Italy. In a strait jacket if needed. Then I'll lock— Hang on."

The door is ripped open. I fall into Tommaso's arms with a squeal.

"You will get yours later."

"How... How did you know?"

"You never ran that bath, *tesoro*." He slaps my butt. "You were not supposed to hear any of that. Now be a good girl, even though I know it's very hard for you. Bend over for me."

I glance into the kitchen where Stephano observes us with interest.

"Not in front of—"

"Yes, in front of. Ten. And one for every second extra you disobey."

I bend forward in the next moment and place my palms against the wall. Tommaso strokes along my thigh, up, up, his touch making me hot and tingly, then he smacks me.

Six. Seven. Eight. Nine. Ten.

The last few are lighter, more playful. "Now, run along. Bath, and get yourself ready for me. I'm cross. My work was interrupted. My brother is an *idiota*, and you disobey me." He leans in and puts his mouth to my ear. "I need your sweet pussy, and I'll fuck you hard."

Yes please. I'm suddenly grateful to Stephano for showing up.

No one in history has ever run a bath, shaved her

legs, brushed her teeth, and stroked rose scented lotion faster than I do.

"You grew up with your father, no? Just the two of you. What was it like?" Tommaso has one of his days when he's full of questions.

It's Sunday, and for once we can lie a little longer in bed. He's not off to some grim 'work', and my store is closed. His arms and legs are wrapped around me, and I feel safe, almost... loved... in our cocoon.

It always hurts, still after so many years, to think of my mother and that I never got to know her. It's so unfair. There were so many times when I needed her.

"My father was a good man," I say. "Full of stories. He loved books. He was a loner. I don't think he ever really got over my mother's death.

"My father killed my mother."

Chapter Fourteen

Carrie

"Oh my God, *what*?" My stomach plummets, and an intense ache spreads through my chest. Poor Tommaso. "He killed her? What happened? Where's he now?"

"I work with him."

My mouth falls open. I try to process this. "That's insane. You must hate him."

Tommaso tuts and shrugs. "Mother had struck a deal with the authorities. Less time in prison. She wanted to come back to her children. To me and my brothers. She betrayed my father."

"You must hate him so much."

He is silent, purses his lips. "It's life in the Crew, little one. Lives are not valued the same everywhere, and we all believe we will meet in Heaven."

I sputter. "I think I would hate your father."

"My father had Mother executed in her sleep. She never knew. It was merciful, and he mourned her for a very long time. He has never remarried. If he hadn't taken care of it, someone else in the organization would have, and they would have tortured her for days, maybe weeks. There is no mercy for traitors. He did all he could to protect her. After, he set our house on fire. He didn't need to cover any evidence, but he didn't want anyone else to get to touch her. Also, he didn't want to set foot there ever again. Tragically enough, Stephano came home from school at the exact wrong moment. He ran inside and tried to save Mother. Father almost couldn't save him in time."

"That's why—" I gesture to my face.

Tommaso nods. "He never forgave Father."

"Did he tell on him? Is that why he lives here?"

"No. He's loyal to the clan, but yes, he left us, and he's been living a destructive life ever since. How do you say... Burning his candle."

"I think I would fear your way of life."

"You would never live my life, little one. You would be protected."

"How can anyone be protected from something like that? What if you decided I couldn't live any longer? Would you kill me?"

Tommaso hugs me closer. "I have hundreds of ruthless men who obey me. My family rules a kingdom worthy of a *principessa* like you, with your light and your laugh. You will always be safe with me."

"But what if I betrayed you?"

His eyes darken, making me want to shrink back, but I force myself to stay.

"Why would you? You would never be involved with anything incriminating. I have learned my lesson. Mother was part of the business. She knew everything. That would never happen to you."

"But would you kill me if you thought I had wronged you?"

"No." His voice has taken on a dangerous tone, but I push on.

"Would your dad?"

"You ask too many questions."

"Would he? Your brothers? Your life seems so cold and cruel. How can you even ask me to move across the world? For that?"

"Not for that. For me. That is where I belong, and you belong by my side."

"Please, don't ask me to do that. You're killing me. Can't you stay here?"

"My life is in *Italia*. I want you with me."

"I have my store. It's my life, my heritage. I can't just up and leave."

The muscles on the sides of his jaw clenches and unclenches. He looks terrifying, but I know I'm safe with him. He lives a brutal life, but he always takes care of me. He won't raise his hand against me in anger. I stroke his cheek, feel the muscles work.

"How old were you?" I ask.

"When?"

"When your mom...passed?"

"Six. I was six"

"Oh my God. I was six, too. Do you remember it well?"

His face turns somber, naked and vulnerable. "Clear as yesterday, *tesoro*."

Tommaso

It probably used to be a fancy house once. Now it's a shack with stained walls and with layers of dirt on the floors. The cigarette smoke hangs like a thick fog in the air.

"Is she a good fuck?"

I spin around and scan the men at the table, looking for whoever spoke. Dee, a bald man with bad teeth and a tattoo of an eagle covering half his head looks at me challengingly.

"Whose business is it who I fuck?" I say, meeting his stare. He's high on something. Cocaine. Heroin. Meth. I've lost count of how much and what these people snort, smoke, or inject. I also don't care. Them killing themselves is their own business. I do care that they've taken notice where I sleep, though. It doesn't sit right with me. I don't like anyone's attention on Carrie, except mine.

Dee spits on the floor and stands. I shift my interest to where everyone has their hands, making sure no one goes for a gun, then I meet his gaze and wait.

"It becomes my business when the chick's not paying up."

"What are you talking about? You're getting what she owes."

"Yeah, but from your fucking pockets."

I shrug. "Money is money. It's none of your business where it comes from. She's giving me my due. You get yours." I cringe inside from dirtying what I have with Carrie, but it's necessary.

Dee moves in and tries to stare me down, which is funny, since he's about half a foot shorter. "I'm making it my business," he snarls. "Get your head out of her pussy long enough to do your fucking job."

I force a calm I'm not feeling. "Are you not pleased with my work?" I know they are. I haven't failed them. I also know they've been looking for a reason to pick a fight since I got here. I can only assume Stephano did something to irk them. I wouldn't be surprised. Being annoying is one of his best qualities.

Dee spits again, right in front of my feet. I look at him, then around the room. Seven men. Do they not know I could kill them all within a minute? I raise my eyebrows, waiting for an answer. Dee spreads his arms and smirks, then he goes back to his chair.

I narrow my eyes, then I turn and leave. My days are hard, and my working hours are long, but I keep my head down, do what I'm told, and count the days until I'm done. From now on I'll have to look out for Dee. If he has his eyes on Carrie, it's not good.

We live in a candy-colored bubble of coffee and books, long walks, talks, and marathon sex. I have tidied up her house, her life, and her store. I know everything about her business, and I've helped her streamline her accounting, even though I have yet to learn about the mess that is US tax law. Yes, I like control.

Carrie has settled by my side, fitting me like the most exclusive tailored suit, like a missing piece of my puzzle. I have barged into her life and made her follow my lead, my rules, and this might not be what she had wanted if I had asked. But I didn't ask. I loathe asking for anything. I take, by force, if needed. If that's not enough, I use more force.

I have fought my whole life to feel safe, to build walls that no one can penetrate, to make up for the loss of young Tommaso's innocence. Little Carrie has put a chink in that armor, and the cracks grow, day by day, spreading like a fine web across my polished surface. She wants in. I want to let her in. My fear of becoming vulnerable keeps us staggering along that fine line.

I haven't become who I am by being a trusting person. I can take her, simply take her. I have toyed with the idea more than once. When the day comes, I'll throw her in the car, carry her inside the plane, and take her with me.

That would destroy everything.

I know it.

Despite who I am, and what I do, despite the way I forced myself into her life, I see faith in her eyes, in her manners. She believes there's good in me, and that little part, the boy who lost his mother, the boy inside who sometimes just needs a caring stroke along his cheek, fights the monster who wants to ravage and ruin. He's strong, and he grows stronger the more time I spend with her. She feeds a light I thought I had lost a long time ago.

There's true tenderness in my chest when I think of my little American girl. I want to do right by her. I just don't know how.

Chapter Fifteen

Tommaso

Stealing her away to Italy isn't the way, and time moves too fast, it seems. Soon, I'll be out of options if she doesn't come around.

"But I have my life here, Tommaso! Sugar Princess, my friends, Cookie. I can't go to Italy."

I laugh, but it sounds bitter rather than joyful. "What friends?"

She looks hurt, and I regret the words as soon as they leave my mouth. I gesture to Cookie, who is bouncing along the sidewalk, stopping time and time again to sniff disgusting things. "Your neighbor can find someone else to care for Cookie during the day. Or adapt her life to the fact that she has a dog. It's not your responsibility."

"I love Cookie." Carrie looks at her feet, her

shoulders slumped. *Crack.* My armor crumbles. She's hurting. I hurt her. What began as a mad whim, then continued as a game, has become real. These are real emotions. In her. In me.

I never thought I'd have them.

But I will never live in the US.

"I'll buy you another dog. I'll buy you ten. I'll give you everything you could ever wish for. I will help you open a bookstore in Milan."

She scoffs and kicks a pebble that shoots across the sidewalk and hits a parked car. Carrie mumbles a curse and picks up her pace. I grab her arm.

"Hey."

She looks up at me. Tears glitter in her eyelashes. My heart softens in a second. "I'm sorry, Tommaso." Her lower lip trembles. "I don't know what to do. It's breaking my heart."

I pull her into my arms.

Crack.

"I'm sorry you're hurting, *tesoro*."

"I'm afraid."

"I know."

"I need time."

"There's not a lot of time left."

"You can stay longer?"

Under no circumstances will I stay in this country beyond the extent of my contract. "I'm needed back home."

"I'm needed here. Sugar Princess is my life, it's

my heritage, it's all I have left of my family. You always talk about family and how important it is. You must understand."

I hug her close, reveling in how, like always, she molds her body to mine. "I'm your family. You will have a new one. They will love you. You will have aunts and uncles, brothers, and sisters. Everyone's dying to meet you."

"Tommaso..." Her voice breaks. "You've talked about me? With your family?"

I kiss the top of her head and then stroke the tears off her cheeks. "Let's get you to work, *principessa*. We will talk about this later."

Of course, I have talked about her. I can't think of anything but her. Carrie Ellerbrock has my whole heart.

Carrie

The front doorbell of my shop rings. It's almost closing time, and I smile to myself as I climb the steps, two at a time, to go meet Tommaso.

It's not him, though.

In the center of the room stand four men I would have crossed the sidewalk to avoid, even if it had been on a crowded street in the middle of the day—tattoos, thick gold chains, filth, bruises, scars, and missing teeth. I take them in as I back up, glancing at the clock, praying time will run faster and that Tommaso will be here really soon.

"Can I help you? We're just about to close." I hope they'll believe I'm not alone. My heart slams, and my mouth is suddenly paper dry.

A tall, gangly man in his upper twenties slants toward me. He's bald, with a huge tattoo of an eagle on the side of his head. It's hideous. I think of Tommaso's tattoos and wonder about the meaning of this one.

"So, this is his little fuckbuddy?" He moves in behind me and puts his mouth to my ear, making chills run down my neck. "Tell your Italian friend that he's failed his fucking mission. You hear me? We'll get him, and we'll get his fucking bro, too." He grabs my ass, making me jump and yelp.

The other three men have pulled out plastic cans from the large bags by their feet and have spread out. After screwing open the cans, they begin pouring a liquid along the walls and on the books. A sharp stench of gasoline reaches my nostrils.

"No! Please!" I try to move, try to reach them, but the man behind me grabs me and wraps an arm around my neck.

"Light it up, guys! We'll show the fucker we're not playing around! This is what happens when you don't fucking pay."

"Please! No!" I scream, and then my pleas turn into a wordless wail as they set Princess on fire.

I'm pushed to my knees, and in the next moment the men have disappeared out the front door. Before me, the flames catch on, rise, devour everything that is me and my life.

Chapter Sixteen

Tommaso

Something makes me speed up my motorcycle past all limits. There's a tug inside me, pulling me to her, screaming at me that I need to keep her safe. The faraway sound of sirens increases by the second, and the smell of smoke gets stronger the closer I get to Carrie. It doesn't have to be her store, or even in her block, but instinct twists my insides into an inferno of raw fear.

I arrive outside Sugar Princess at the same time as the fire fighters begin to roll out their hoses and shout their orders. Heat and flames have cracked all the large front windows and already lick the façade on the second floor. I don't bother with the front entrance—it's engulfed—and instead leap into the little alley behind the building, take the stairs to the basement level in a few strides, where I find a distraught Cookie who barks at the open door to the bakery in the back. I unhook the chain to let her loose. Smoke billows out the door, but there are no flames. I tear off my suit jacket and hold it over my mouth and nose as I crouch under the smoke and run inside. My heart slams in fear of losing what I've just found.

"Carrie!" I roar. The light is still on, but it's getting darker by the second as the smoke intensifies. "Carrie!" My eyes sting and tears well up.

I look up the long, narrow set of stairs to the office, praying she isn't up there. The wall reflects the orange glow from the fire in the store, and the roar from the hell that has broken loose is deafening.

"Carrie!" I take a step before I hesitate in the black smoke that steals all the air.

A cough from upstairs, then a faint voice. "Tommaso!"

My life is nothing. Hers is everything. There is no hesitation. I run up, toward the flames and the heat, toward the only woman I will ever care about. I can't lose her. I won't.

She comes stumbling, her arms full of books, sooty, her eyes huge, reddened, frightened, tears and snot streaming down her face.

"Tommaso!"

"I'm here, *bella, tesoro*, my love."

I catch her, cradle her against my chest, and run

back down. There's no oxygen left, but my willpower is stronger than my need to breathe. We stumble out in the backyard. Carrie falls to her hands and knees and throws up, then she rolls over on her back, every breath wheezing.

I hold her hair away from the vomit, stroke her forehead. "What happened?" It clearly wasn't a kitchen malfunction.

"They said I hadn't paid," she gasps.

They.

I know who 'they' are without hesitation.

Everything inside me goes black with instant, primal rage. My beast roars and throws himself at his restraints. That bald meth-head with an inflated ego has interfered with my life for the last time. I don't need more details.

'They' are dead. They just don't know it yet.

Crack.

My armor is no more. Almost losing this woman, so new in my life, and still my everything, tears down my last wall. I want her. I need her. I don't know how to live the rest of my years if I don't get to have her with me. I'm just getting to know her. I refuse to lose this.

"Come." My lungs burn, but my blood boils hotter. I have tunnel vision. I need Carrie to be cared for, then I'll arm myself to the teeth and wipe out the pretend gangsters who have laid claim to this part of the city. With Cookie by my feet, I carry my sooty *principessa* up the stairs in the backyard, into the alley, back out on the street.

"Help! We need help here!"

Two firefighters drop what they have and rush to meet us. I stand with her until they have put an oxygen mask over her nose and mouth, until I know she's receiving care, then I kiss her forehead.

"I'll be back, *tesoro*. I have some things to take care of."

I see the pain and the worry in her eyes. She knows what I need to do, and she might disagree, but she understands.

"Not for me," she whispers.

I kiss her again. "For me, then."

"Be careful, my Tommaso."

"I'll be back."

I'll be back after I make sure that no one harms Carrie Ellerbrock ever again.

I have exactly one gun and one knife. I plan to equip myself while I kill the boys playing criminals. They all carry semi-automatics. It'll rip them apart appropriately, sever limbs, tear up chests. When I'm done, even their mothers won't recognize them. Fury rages inside me like it has never done before. I grew up with violence. It's in my blood; killing is second nature. As I've matured, I've learned to contain it. I don't resort to it whenever someone has wronged me.

Not slight wrongs of the kind I felt were important the first couple of decades in my life.

This is not slight. This threatens the existence of someone I love. Yes, love. I've known it for a while, felt it. I fear what I'm about to do threatens it as much. This kind of life isn't one to offer my *principessa*, and yet, selfishly, it's exactly what I plan to do.

On the way over, I pass a gas station and buy a gift. Something suitable, given their own preferred methods.

I park my motorcycle a block from the dilapidated mansion and grab my stuff. It's evening. They should be in, at least enough of them, slouching on old sofas, playing their PlayStations. Someone stays on guard, often with pupils dilated from their drug of choice. My family does deal with them, cater to the masses with their insatiable weaknesses. We're no angels; we have no scruples.

Again, what am I pulling my *tesoro* into?

One man stands by the entrance, smoking, his stance relaxed. I walk right up to him and tilt my head in a greeting he responds to without a second of hesitation. *Idiota.*

I walk up to him and bury my knife in his throat, my hands over his mouth to silence any moan. I hold him and kneel with him as he sags to the ground. While he still twitches in his last moments of death, I find his gun, secure it, and put it in my pocket, then I open the can with gasoline, douse the wooden door and porch and light it up.

With the flames licking the door, I crouch and run around the house. Judging from the shouts, they've already discovered the fire. I kick in the back door and shoot the two first men I see. The shots will alert the house, but I've got a semi now.

I hide in an alcove and wait. Two of the junkies come running. I take them down and hang the automatic rifle over my shoulder then secure the other guy's gun, putting it in another pocket.

I expect about five more, and I still haven't seen the bald, skinny man with all the tattoos. He's my number one priority.

From the front of the house, through the corridor, comes increasingly blackening smoke.

Distraction and cutting off the escape route. Two flies in one hit.

No one else comes my way, so I begin to move again. In the kitchen, I find two men, stuffing money and bags with white content—cocaine, or heroin— into bags. They're a little quicker and throw themselves behind the kitchen island. This results in a shootout. I make sure to cover my back as I move toward them, firing relentlessly, spraying the room, and completely destroying the cupboards. I get one man. Behind me, another appears in the door. He doesn't stand a chance, but then a bullet nicks my shoulder. I ignore the pain and roll forward. Finding the last man before me, I shoot him while I'm still moving.

I secure the rest of the first floor, then return to the living room, aiming for the hallway, now filled with thick smoke, but I don't get that far. Before me stands the leader.

"What the fuck's wrong with you, man?" he yells then fires a few shots in my general direction before he dodges behind a couch.

"You shouldn't have come for what's mine," I roar as I approach him. I shoot up the couch, fabric and stuffing flying. The young wannabe crime boss yelps with every hit. He jumps up and sprays bullets in my direction. I dodge them, then I charge him. With the squirming skinny weasel beneath me, I slam his gun arm against the floor until he loses his grip. I shove it away, then slam my fist against his throat. Gasping for air, his face beet red, he still tries to go for the gun.

I hit his face. And again. And again. Thrown back in time, I do what I do best. I revert to the monster my Carrie doesn't need in her life. She's love and light, while I'm terror and death. How could I?

The shit on the floor is no more. No breaths. No signs of life.

No one to hurt my *principessa* ever again.
Except me and my world.

Chapter Seventeen

Carrie

Every breath sets off an ache deep in my lungs, and my windpipe feels as if someone went over it with a steel brush. But I'll heal.

Physically.

I spend one night in the hospital, with a dark shadow guarding me. He comes in somewhere around midnight, still reeking of smoke from the fire. I can't believe they allowed him in, and I fear to imagine what he said to compel them to let him stay.

His posture is stiff, his face grim. I will never want to know where he went and what he did after he left me on the sidewalk outside my store, but even in the dimly lit room I see the bloodstains on his shirt sleeve.

They release me, and Tommaso drives me home

in a black van I haven't seen before. I won't ask about that one either. My mind is blown, my energy spent. My physical pain has nothing on the agony of seeing my father's store burn. I managed to save a few of his favorite books, memories of my childhood years, the picture of me and him that sat on the desk. And the tiara.

"Are you okay?"

We've barely talked. I'm afraid I'll scream if I open my mouth. I shake my head and hug my knees to my chest.

"How can I help?"

The wail inside me builds despite my efforts. *You're leaving in a couple of weeks! You've opened my heart, and now you're ripping it from my chest! I have nothing left!*

"You can't," I finally grit out.

"The store is gone. I'm sorry."

Hearing it said out loud hurts as if I've lost my father all over again.

"I don't know what to do." I rock back and forth to try to comfort myself.

"Let me take care of you, Carrie. You have nothing left here. With the bookshop gone, what will you do, *tesoro*? Come with me, back to Italy."

It slams into me like a freight train. I turn my head slowly. His mouth falls open, and he shakes his head, as if warning me from saying what's about to come out of my mouth, but I can't stop it. All the signs are there. The possessive behavior, his need for control. He wants something, he makes sure it happens.

"Did you do this? Did you tell them to burn my dad's store?" The betrayal rips me in two. I can't breathe. "Let me out!" I try to open the passenger door, but the lock won't open. "Open the door. Stop the car. Let me out! You piece of shit!" I kick at the dashboard and push at the door, then I curl in on myself. I don't want to be here anymore. "You said I was safe! You lied to me! My father's store—" The ache inside eats up the last words.

He is too quiet. We speed toward my neighborhood. Finally, I dare a glance in his direction and recoil from the look on his face. I have never seen anyone look so hurt before in my life.

I did that.

He pulls up right outside my front door and comes around the car to help me out. I push at his hand, but he's not having it, and I'm too weak to object harder. My skin longs for his touch even when I'm angry. I need his care, his love. I don't want him to be upset, but I don't know how to take back what I just said.

"Tommaso... I'm sorry. I don't—"

"It's nothing to talk about. You're upset. I know you don't mean that. You need to rest." He scoops me up and cradles me to his chest, carrying me all the way up to the bedroom on the second floor. He feels different. Stiff. Angry.

"Do... do you want to punish me?" My cheeks burn. I don't know what to do, how to mend this.

"Absolutely not," he says, and that's when I know something is really wrong. I choke down the sobs that want to escape, swallow against the agony in my chest and climb into bed, allowing him to tuck me in.

When I come to, I don't know if it's still today, or how much time has passed. Tommaso sits by my bed, his legs crossed, his hands resting on his lap. Next to me stands a tray with a glass of juice and a ham-and-cheese sandwich.

"I could force you to come with me, *principessa*. I could wrap you up, muffle your screams, throw you over my shoulder and take you with me. Who would stop me? Who would dare stop me? But my world is dark and cold. It can be terrifying, and that's not how I want this. I want you to *want* to come with me. I need you to be brave. I don't want to fight. I want to relax. I want to come home to my warm, willing girl, waiting for me, eager to see me, eager to please. So, I bid you farewell. I don't play games. I have no patience for them. People get hurt. I get hurt, and so will you. Farewell, Miss Ellerbrock."

"You... you have two more weeks here."

His smile is grim and doesn't reach his eyes. "My contract here can be considered... void. Stephano has nothing to worry about anymore. Not him. Not you."

"Oh."

He's breaking my heart. I knew he would the moment I saw him, and it's happening now.

I want to hold on to him, beg him to stay, my big, bad Italian mobster, but he would be unhappy here, and as much as I am selfish, I also care too much about this strange man who has given me more than I could have ever asked for in the few short months we've known each other.

Swallowing, I try to come up with an answer, a greeting that will tell him everything I feel, everything he has awoken, but I'm frozen in pain, unable, terrified of the lonely life that awaits me, knowing that I'll never find anyone who can see right through to my core like Tommaso.

Tears well up in my eyes. "I'm sorry for what I said. I don't believe that."

He bows his head. "I know, *tesoro*, and I accept your apology. Live a good life, Carrie Ellerbrock." He stands, presses his lips against my forehead, and then he turns and leaves.

Just like that, he's gone.

Chapter Eighteen

Carrie

I own my house again. I have no loans, and with the insurance money from the burnt-down Sugar Princess, I'll manage financially until I know what I want to do with the rest of my life.

Thing is, what I want might not be an option anymore.

It's been two agonizing weeks. I should try to rebuild the store or find another job. I still want to work with books, but my heart isn't here. I can't function without Tommaso. I miss him so much that I can't eat or sleep. I take long walks with Cookie, in secret telling her goodbye because it hurts too much to say it out loud. I google Italian translations of every word I can think of, and blanch at how difficult it seems to learn another language. Do I start over at almost thirty? What life awaits me there? What life do I have here?

'I want to relax. I want to come home to my warm, willing girl, waiting for me, eager to see me, eager to please.'

I want nothing more.

So, I do the only thing left to do. The only thing that might mend my broken heart.

"Lu-ci-ano. San Francisco. He... he probably"—I cough—"works in organized crime. There's also a connection with someone called Nathan, or Christian Russo. Or both. That's all I have."

The silence on the other end is deafening. Then he clears his throat. "Got it. I'll get back to you, ma'am."

There are too many people living in this country, and finding a person if you're a nobody with no contacts can be ridiculously hard. Finding a mob boss who doesn't want to be found is impossible. Finally, I've had to resort to finding a private investigator who'll do the search for me since no mysterious mobster by the name of Luciano seems to exist.

That one time he mentioned his uncle is my only link to Tommaso. That, and when I listened to him and his brother. Trying to find my man in Milano, Italy, is an option I pass on before I even consider it.

At least for now. It's a foreign country, I don't know how I should go about that.

He left. He really left me. Somehow, I thought he'd give me an email address, or a cell phone number, or something, but he just disappeared. The phone he had when he was here—I found it on the kitchen counter next to my house keys. The vision was a whole new level of gutting.

Three days pass by. More of the same.

Wake.

Try to eat.

Cry.

Walk Cookie.

Try to eat.

Cry.

Then...

My phone rings.

"Carrie." There's always a little hope inside that it might be him, but it's crushed when the voice isn't right. It has a thick, rolling accent. Harsh.

"Miss Ellerbrock?"

"That's me."

"I've heard you've been looking for someone."

Everything goes still. My heart thunders in my chest as if I have been running. "Who's this?"

"My name is Ivan Sokolov, I work for Mr. Luciano Salvatore."

Tommaso

Life goes back to normal.

Or it should, but it doesn't.

Not in the least.

Many things happen, and I seem to end up in the middle of everything.

My *idiota* of a brother is free from the clutches of the American gangsters.

Except he's gone and done the most *stupido* thing he could have ever done. He's brought a woman back home to *Milan*. A black-haired beauty with dark, expressive, almond-shaped eyes.

Her name is Angela Russo, and we suddenly have a small war on our hands. Stealing away a Mafia princess from a competing *famiglia* isn't the brightest idea. The Russo clan isn't known for taking insults lightly, and this is no small thing. It doesn't take long before we have a whole bunch of their worst enforcers on our doorstep.

But any Italian worth his salt honors *Amore*. Love.

I've had my hands full with family business, but nothing can distract me from the knowledge that I've let my own love go.

I dig up everything I can about Carrie Ellerbrock. Turns out I already knew her. I've never felt such a connection with anyone who wasn't already family. That's when I realize it's what she is.

Carrie is family. She belongs *here,* by my side, in my bed, no matter if she realizes it.

I perform work with unnecessary cruelty. I lash out around me in my frustration.

Finally, I've had it.

I make all necessary preparations, so she'll feel at home. I know what she likes. I know her food preferences, the clothes she wears, what colors she decorated her home with. I know her stuffed animals, her makeup, her shampoo and conditioner—we're not in the US, but I find the same scents from other brands —exclusive brands. Carrie was a retail girl. Not anymore.

I prepare a wardrobe with tight blouses with plunging necklines, short, wide skirts, and ballerina-style shoes, a little library, she'll sleep with me, obviously, and I'll let her put her own spin on our bedroom. I find a few choices of stores, some empty, some... not, if she wants to open a bookstore in *Milan.*

Then I reserve a flight.

I'm picking up my *principessa,* and fuck if I'll give her a choice.

That's not even a question.

Chapter Nineteen

Carrie

Everything is ready.

Ivan Sokolov was oddly helpful, but I'm not complaining.

I have an address in Milano. I have a passport and ticket. My bags are packed. I have a phone number for Tommaso, but I haven't dared to call him. It's a mad plan, but I'm hoping he won't throw me out if I just show up on his doorstep. I want to show him that I'm dedicated. I don't want him to talk me out of coming. I don't want to be reasonable. If I travel across the globe, and it turns out to be for nothing, then at least I gave it my everything.

I'm nervous, filled with trepidation and hope. With my hairbrush in one hand and a long list of things I need to do in the other, I bounce down the stairs. I'm leaving tomorrow. I've never been so ready for anything. I've never been so organized. I thank him for that. He made me want to do better, be better, and no matter where we end up, I'll always honor what he taught me.

I stop dead, a feeling of déjà vu washing over me. A tall, dark figure stands in the middle of my kitchen, in his hands my ticket and passport. He looks up and my knees fold. I grab the doorpost and hold on, thinking I'll faint any moment.

"T-Tommaso?"

"Going somewhere?"

"You came back!" My heart somersaults. I drop the list of notes and the hairbrush and throw myself in his arms. "You came back!"

Tommaso hugs me close, tight, tight, his scent, his strength, his very existence making everything right that was wrong.

"Seems you're leaving, though, *bella*."

"I'm..." My cheeks heat up. What if he'll admonish me? What if he won't want me to go? "I was coming to you."

"To Italy? Really?"

He doesn't sound the least surprised. He sounds like he's teasing me.

Hold on a minute...

"Why are you here?"

"A little bird whispered in my ear that a certain *principessa* was going on a long journey all by herself."

"I told Ivan not to tell you!"

Tommaso laughs. "And who do you think he's more loyal to?"

'Family is everything.'

I groan. "I didn't know if you still wanted me to come. I was gonna call you when I landed."

He strokes my hair and plants a kiss on the top of my head. "I could have been on the other side of the world. Don't ever do that again. Plan ahead, and never be afraid to ask me anything."

"I won't. I promise."

"Now that's my good, good girl."

My heart feels like it's bursting with joy and pride. When Tommaso calls me good, then everything is set right again.

"I'm so sorry for what I said. Was that why you left? I was beside myself. I can't blame anyone else, the words came out of my mouth, but I didn't think. I know you wouldn't hurt me. I know you would never burn—"

He puts a finger to my lips, and I snap my mouth closed. He smiles and shakes his head. "It hurt some, but I knew you were in a dark place. I left because both you and I needed to clear our heads, little one. I felt... I wasn't entirely in control. I could never stay away. That was clever of you, remembering Luciano's name. And, apparently, the Russos, you bad girl"

I blush. "It was all I had. Are you saying you were coming back?"

"Most certainly. Being away from you felt like trying to breathe underwater." His eyes glitter, making my insides ache with want. "Are you ready to leave?"

"What? Now?"

He nods.

I look around me. I am, actually. I'm very ready.

"My ticket is for—"

He tuts and shakes his head. "I have my own jet."

"Your own? Isn't that expensive?"

"It's necessary when I need to be somewhere fast, and right now I need you bent over my kitchen table, with your ass bared accepting your punishment for what you've put me through these last weeks. Fast."

And just like that, he's got me. I'm his. Now and forever.

"I'm sorry."

"*Tesoro*, I'm never letting you go now. You must know this."

"I'm not going anywhere."

He smiles, then he laughs, and it's the most beautiful sound in the world.

"I love you, Carrie Ellerbrock."

"I love you right back, Tommaso Vittelli. I learned..."—I swallow, hoping I'll please him—"to make panna cotta for you. It's only what I found online but... I wanted to surprise you, but I can never keep my mouth shut. Can I do that? When we get there? Will you let me make you sweet pudding?"

My big brute, my gangster, my caretaker, my Italian teddy bear, takes my hand and then he scoops me up in his arms as if I weigh nothing. "*Mia dolce principessa*, we'll ask Grandmother to teach you the old recipe. I'd love to taste your pudding." He kisses the side of my neck, little pecks that leave a trail of goose bumps. "I will taste your everything. I'm taking you home. You will never be alone again. There's a huge family who can't wait to meet you, and they will, after I'm done with you."

I bury my head in his chest. "Thank you. Thank you, my love."

His beautiful smile would be reward enough, but bundled up in his strong arms, I know there will be many more rewards coming up.

My reward begins on the breathtakingly sleek, sexy, very comfortable plane.

Or is it punishments?

I can't tell.

We make the flight attendant blush more than once while we cross an ocean of water.

"I had no idea there is so much water."

Tommaso laughs. "Our planet's surface consists of seventy percent water."

"Seventy? Wow." I press my nose against the window, still seeing nothing but sun on a cloudless sky and a vast glittering water surface below us. Then I moan. Again. I have nothing on but bra and panties. My bra sits askew, and my panties are pushed to the side.

Tommaso fingers my clit, circles it with his skilled fingers until I swell, until I ache and burn for him. He grabs me, spins me around and then throws me on the plush, beige couch.

"How do you know?" I ask on a half gasp, half squeal.

He stares at me, incredulously, as he hovers above me, his thick cock hard and eager. His pants are bunched around his ankles, his shirt a half-buttoned mess, displaying a thick dusting of black chest hair. He looks wild. My kind of wild. "Do they not teach geography in American schools?"

I scowl. "Of course, they do. But... perhaps a bit America centric."

Tommaso is silent a little too long.

I add, because I have to, "When will we fall off the edge?"

He looks so horrified I burst out in laughter. "I'm pulling your leg."

He snickers. "I will teach you, *cara*. And I will give you something *else* to pull." Then he grabs my wrists, slams up my arms against the cushion, nudges my thighs wider apart, and thrusts inside in one rough move. "I will teach you. For every wrong answer, a spank. For every right... ten."

I laugh in delight as he pounds in me.

He knows me too well, my beloved gangster.

I believe I'll love it in *Italia*.

Epilogue

Carrie

My love lives in a castle.

It hides behind a cast iron fence with pointy bars —the tips arrow-shaped and gilded—behind perfectly cut bushes, a lush lawn, and large trees— behind a huge gate that slides to the side with seemingly no one to man it—behind almost-hidden surveillance cameras.

Driving up along the driveway takes several minutes. It's so long and winding that at first, I don't even see the house.

And then it appears before us. Huge. Three stories high, white, several wings, surrounded by more of the garden which seems to be made for kings and queens.

I gasp and grab Tommaso's arm, shaking it. "Is this it? Is this your home?"

We sit in the back of a very silent Mercedes with oddly green-tinted, thick windows. Reinforced, Tommaso told me. The thought of why sent a shiver through me, which he immediately picked up on. *'Don't worry,* tesoro. *Your life from now on will be exquisite food, a beautiful home, books, travel, and lots and lots of spanks. No darkness for you.'*

Taking in the mansion, I choose to believe him. Good things await me here.

"Is this ours?"

"Ours is the south wing, with a view of the garden and the lake. You can't see it from here."

"A lake? There's a *lake*? Can I swim in it?"

He laughs his rich, dark laugh. "Of course. It's very clean."

"I have so many questions, Tommaso."

The car stops, the driver opens our door, and Tommaso helps me out. I make a move toward the trunk, but Tommaso tuts and takes my hand in his. He guides me toward a huge portal that leads through a vault and into an inner yard.

It has four façades, all with two sets of doors, except the one opposite the gate, which is the one we're moving toward. It has one set of giant double wooden doors.

Yeah, I have *so* many questions, but my mind blanks out. There are servants, cooks, gardeners, high ceilings adorned with paintings, staircases, chamber after chamber after chamber.

"I will get lost," I say and clutch his hand.

"I will be by your side until you make *Casa* Vittelli and *Milan* your home, *tesoro*."

We finally stop by a door.

"Is this it?" I ask.

He nods. "This is where our quarters begin."

My heart throbs harder. I want to like it. I want to *love* it. "I'm ready."

He squeezes my hand, and then we enter.

Like the rest of the house, the decoration is dark, old fashioned. Wooden floors that creak beneath our weight, deep windowsills, where I can easily fit with a book. I run to a window and take in the view of the sunny garden and the glittering surface of the lake, then I spin around.

"It's so beautiful! It's so quiet."

"It is also very soundproof," says Tommaso with a wicked grin. He takes my hand again. "Come."

Behind a door at the end of the corridor is a small library, the colors lighter, a huge pink armchair by the single window. I gasp and dart inside, dragging the tips of my fingers along the spines as I make a lap.

"This is for you."

I turn with a gasp. "For me?"

"I will give you everything you need. Let me show you the bedroom."

And right then and there I know he will truly give me *everything* I need.

I will not be able to sit tonight without a stinging reminder of our first afternoon in my new home. I will be presented to his father and brothers with a tender, blushing butt, but it's *so* going to be worth it.

Tommaso works a lot and is gone for hours, sometimes days, on end. It's more than fine. Our reunions are always making up for it, and I have a never-ending house, garden, and city to explore. There's a whole new language to learn, and I also have a puppy to play with.

I call her Cookie, because why not, and also, her fur has brown dots like a chocolate chip cookie, so there's that.

We are looking at a place for me to set up a new Sugar Princess, but until then I have a lot of free time.

And oh my God, does this house have secrets.

I all too often hear the names 'Russo', and 'Salvatore' in discussions between the brothers, the father, and other men around them, and then they always go quiet when they realize I'm listening. I know the scary, scarred brother—Stephano—has gone and done something unforgivable, something about another *principessa*. His own *principessa*, Angela

Russo. I hope I get to meet her one day. She sounds interesting.

And then I hear the servants whisper. I make out the words 'sleeping' and 'woman'. Of course, I have to check this out.

The castle has myriad secret passageways, doors hidden behind paintings, musty old staircases. Me and Cookie explore every single one we can find.

In a wing on the other side of the house, the one belonging to Tommaso's brother Antonio, I find a sleeping beauty.

Or... unconscious.

Her blond hair is neatly braided, her face pale. There's a fading bruise on her forehead, and she's lying on one side of the huge bed in Antonio's master bedroom. It's all pretty creepy.

"Why is there an unconscious woman in your brother's bed?"

"Some questions are better unasked," says Tommaso.

"But... who is she? Is she his wife? There's no ring on her—"

"*Tesoro*. You are too curious, you bad girl."

I swallow and wait. I know what's coming.

"And what do I do to bad girls?"

I giggle. Then I burst out in a laugh as he throws me over his shoulder and carries me straight to bed.

I'll crack all the mysteries, but first I'll have my punishment.

Want more Tommaso and Carrie?
BONUS CHAPTER here!
BookHip.com/VWHKZAR

Sugar Princess Bonus Chapter

Love hot Italian mobsters who force feisty heroines to submit? I have the books for you! Find your next sexy dark hero in the **Russo Saga**.

Excerpt from Heat - book 1 in the
Russo Saga:

Nathan

It's the last day of this hot, literally bloody, hell. Diego Garcia is more resilient than anyone would have thought. Nothing could have prepared us for the fact that he isn't speaking. He knows he'll die. We've been at him for two days. He's been beaten to a pulp. Had his nails and a bunch of teeth pulled out, had a few fingers broken. He's been shot through both kneecaps. He has fainted, been brought back to consciousness, waterboarded, fainted again. We thought he died once, and it would have been a major bummer, but he didn't and we kept at it. He's vomited on my shoes and I thought of shooting his face off. It'd have an impact, literally, but also make it difficult for him to talk.

I figured him as just a small-time crook, but he's

turned out to be a real badass. Diego Garcia knows he'll die no matter what and we have no leverage. We simply don't know what more to do with the man, so we switch to plan B.

Señora Maria Garcia.

I do hope he loves his wife enough.

It's boiling hot in the back of the van, even though we've parked it under the large crown of a tree. I'm alone, monitoring the retrieval of Diego's dark beauty of a wife.

Since I left Sydney on the beach it's felt like I have strings attached to her, pulling me back. It drives me crazy. She tells me to fuck off, in somewhat nicer terms, but it's easy to tell she's as hooked on me as I am on her. I itch, and I can't resist scratching it. It'll be over tomorrow anyway.

So, I call her. My cock stirs as I wait for her to pick up. It rings three times, then I hear her breathless voice.

"Yes? Sydney Lewis."

I smile and glance at the monitor before me. They are still waiting outside the Garcia residence, biding their time.

"Hello?" she says, louder.

"What are you wearing?"

She gasps. *"Nathan! You're impossible."*

"No, I'm not. What are you wearing?"

She inhales sharply. Her unspoken objection

hangs between us. Then she decides to play along. Good, good Sydney Lewis. What a gem I found.

"The same sundress." Her voice trembles slightly.

"What do you have on under it?"

I glance at the screen. Everything is under control. I can almost hear Sydney squirm through the receiver.

"White bikini bottoms," she breathes. *"No bra."*

"You are disobeying my direct orders."

"Last time I checked I was under no obligation to do what you say."

Oh, so brave when I'm not near. "Are you trying my patience?" I make my voice stern, ice cold. "Take them off."

I have to adjust my cock which has gotten rock hard in an instant. There's a rustle of fabric from her end and I grin as I rub a hand along my length. I can't allow myself to get off. Not here. But I'll sure as fuck take what I need later. She thinks she's getting away. Think again, Syd.

"They're off," she says breathlessly.

"Good girl. Are you wet?"

"Probably."

"Touch yourself and tell me."

"Yes," she gasps. *"I am."*

"Are you turned on?"

"Yes."

"Touch yourself, rub your fingers up and down

your pussy and think of me pushing inside you. And moan for me, Syd. I want to hear you."

She is quiet a moment but then her breathing changes, gets heavier. A soft moan comes through the phone, then another.

"Push a finger inside."

"Already have," she breathes.

"Did I tell you to?"

"Mmnooo," she answers in a small voice.

"Slap yourself on the cunt, Syd. Hard. You need to be disciplined."

I hear an actual slap and then she cries out. I bend over, my whole body clenching up. I want her so much it hurts. I stroke my twitching cock through my pants. The front of my briefs is getting wet from precum.

"Good girl," I whisper. There's a movement on the monitor and the radio cracks alive in my ear, short orders barked out. There's still no need for me to interact. They can take care of themselves.

"Use your fingers. Fuck yourself. Think of me and fuck yourself."

"Can I touch my clit?" she whispers, gasping.

I think about it for a moment. I want to hear her come. "Yes, you may."

I listen to her breaths getting heavier, quicker. "Are you thinking of me inside you?"

"Yes," she groans.

"Come for me, Sydney. I want to hear you scream."

I stroke myself harder, my mind spinning. I'm gonna fucking come in my pants. That was not my intention. I glance at the screen. They're pushing the woman to the floor, she's flailing helplessly, then they inject her with a sedative and her struggles weaken. Sydney is gasping, making inarticulate sounds. I rub my cock, my groin tensing. Eric holds the woman down as she tries to fight him off. Sydney cries out. The woman finally stills, and her forced submission combined with Sydney's breaths in my ear makes it the hottest fucking thing I've ever experienced. I come so hard I'm almost falling off the chair. I'm sweaty, my heart hammers, and I gasp for air.

"Good girl," I pant and hang up.

HEAT - book 1 in the Russo Saga - a series of dark, sexy interconnected standalone books in a world of organized crime. Dominant anti heroes and feisty heroines in need of both discipline and saving.

- **I Am Eve**
- **Sugar Princess**
- **Break My Chains**
- **Anomaly**
- **Her Vampire Hero**

Pure filth...

- **Honey Trap**
- **Firefighter's Pet**
- **Demon Lust**

For everything Nicolina

BOOKS, SOCIALS, ETC

linktr.ee/nicolinamartin

Acknowledgments

Thank you, my wonderful editor Nerine Dorman, and my cover designer Dani René. Thank you EJ Frost for giving me invaluable advice on this beautiful little story.

www.ingramcontent.com/pod-product-compliance
Lightning Source LLC
LaVergne TN
LVHW091710190726
843493LV00001B/235